ANWAR

ANWAR
War, Love and Country

REJOICE KUR

Library of Congress Control Number: 2022915180
ISBN: Hardcover   978-1-6698-3133-4
                   Softcover   978-1-6698-3132-7
                   eBook   978-1-6698-3131-0

Print information available on the last page.

Rev. date: 08/31/2022

To order additional copies of this book, contact:
Xlibris
AU TFN: 1 800 844 927 (Toll Free inside Australia)
AU Local: (02) 8310 8187 (+61 2 8310 8187 from outside Australia)
www.Xlibris.com.au
Orders@Xlibris.com.au
841068

CONTENTS

A PATRIOT FROM
THE NORTH

When the persuasion to convey a cause becomes an intense charge inevitable to the identity of an individual, the acumen of any daunting reality becomes insignificant. This was the dissident venture that rendered the army officer First Sergeant Anwar FadlAllah Fareed into the deliberate derive to a pursuit and the desire to persist even in the face of condescending circumstances until that is accomplished. For how can a more constructive way be permissive in the recount of a cause masked by the expanse of time be hearkened?

In his endeavours to rise as brave as he could be, he joined the military, bringing along the impartial beliefs of a middle-class Sudanese family where government policies were disputed almost every day at dinner time, and there had always been a subtle drive to a revolution awaiting an awakening. First Sergeant, *raquib awwal* Anwar was incited by his insistent instincts to transpire his sentiments in rage of the realities in a country he had pledged to serve with diligence. But those antagonistic commanders couldn't withstand his opposing views, and he cannot be intrigued to silence.

Neither suppression nor prohibition have blunted his enduring fury. He was sent away to the land he was being trained to fight against in the daunting surge of the civil war. The First Sergeant Anwar sat in the compact cabin of a Lockheed L-100-20 Hercules flanked by the window. At the verge of losing it all, that very land has become his new refuge. A man should not shed tears, a rule he had to comply by from childhood. Tears were burning his eyes. He blinked into the rounded glazed window of the aeroplane to see a blurred view of a colossal area fenced with iron chain links at the far end. That was a draw out to renounce his tears the dispensation of the moment.

He slightly pulled his head from one side to the other, where his fellow commuters sat. The cabin crew were two captains. The plane was a cargo, carrying military support, and only a few military personnel were on board. He had never met any of them before, except for a Lieutenant Colonel, *mugaddum* Tom Nazeer whom he got introduced to on receiving his placement orders. *mugaddum* Tom appeared less talkative, or at least it was not yet time for him to talk. For the rest of his entire duty in town, Tom contributed to most of the critical discourses. They didn't get on the same side, but they congruently protruded a constructive discord along each other's pathways.

It was a quite winter afternoon of the year 1995 when the sound of a landing aeroplane reached the edges of Wau town around a distance of 1,006 kilometres into the South from the capital Khartoum. 'Hamdila ala salama', said a very coarse voice from a person sitting beside who had obviously awaken from a nap. That was the Sudanese phrase implying 'a safe arrival'. Everyone was gazing around in alertness to the time for exit.

Anwar raised his head as he stepped onto the stairs and made his way out of the plane. All around was vastness and quiescence. The only building in sight was a slot white painted chalet, which was the town's airport building. That afternoon the winter sun of the savannah was shimmering over the vicinity with warm caresses of tender breezes. Being a soldier, he was used to the remote and desolate stations. But this place had a different feel with a hint of an anticipation of a transformation. Although he was under restricted orders, the town called him to its first inscriptions, and for him, that spelt home. He walked with the audacity of a squaddie in the face of the unknown. Though he bears the looks of the highly esteemed, he was a detainee, entering a confinement in the town.

That was grip of a mixture of anticipation and dread in a day so unique about his military service. The first sergeant could see how the height of the political and social conflicts can be sensed even in the quietness of the remote town. His attention was drifted to the captains as they communicated with hosting team. The cabin crew were adjusting their tones in a zone where the military had stronger authority, and everyone had to be super vigilant. In facing that, he sensed what interested him the most was the owing simplicity of the surroundings. Right there in his receipt were the preliminary consistency of the town, a hint for inevitable transformation. He was, in fact, facing the definite reality of himself setting out to obtain his newly assigned duty in the town and adequately getting motivated by the colossal change of appealing views.

'This way', he heard the same voice from the plane. It was Tom, his travelling comrade, who had been to the town for many years. Tom was seemingly in his early fifties, short height, and rigid figure with a sombre expression on his face. He was very much acquainted with every procedure in the airport, everything remained ordinary to him. Unlike Anwar, he had travelled the route many times. 'They bring the luggage under that tree', he continued, pointing to a detached woody tree with dense branches standing in the distance.

The luggage was brought on a chariot attached to a 1987 Toyota Hilux. Walking away with his luggage, he got a glimpse of what his journey might bring to his daring pursuit against countless odds. He consigned to his faith with a conviction that all will be good despite any questions and pondering. The surrounding nature was quite appealing to his senses. The structures to the front, as looked beyond the chain-linked fence of the airport, rendered to his sight a limelight of nature's profound spectrum of compressed reddish soil and distant hardwood trees. They climbed another military Toyota, and off they buzzed on a very dusty path to the direction of the town.

Their car took a right turn from a position that divulged a benevolent view of the town he would be residing in for a number of years coming. A clear path centrally located within an extended view of a sequentially lined constructions on both sides of the road depicted a lively aspect of the town. The landscape offered him a tranquil spectacle owing to the flat hilltops and plains and the natural vegetations. He can see the rustic roofs of the town's main quarters amongst dense tropical trees.

At the heart of the residences, a domed pinnacle was visible from the distance. He came to recognise that as one of the monumental churches of the Catholic mission in the country. He later found out many of the military residences in town or in its outskirts belonged to either the church or a learning institution that had been occupied by the military. As they passed by, some more of the town's monuments became very close to sight. A prominent sport compound to one side depicted a serene elevation of an escarpment proportion to inclusiveness. He can even read the signposts written in Arabic.

To the same direction to town on the same side of the road, they proceeded towards a more inundation of passers-by in the haze of the evening sun. A police station built in red laterite stones shone from the reflection of the sun from across the street on the side of a marketplace extending into huts of the neighbourhood. War also had a visible imprint. He could see the vacant stares as the people crossing the streets stood by the side of the road to allow the cars to pass. An undeniable undertone of long-distance walkers carrying baskets, sacks, and children. Bike riders know their path along the step-stone-paced lanes.

They passed a very tinny bridge very substantial to crossing a lengthy gorge that extended into both sides of the road entering an intersection of three-way exits. The road bore an opted view of palpable red soil with augmenting dusts as cars drove by. A calm stream reflecting the painted views of the sky above and the tall trees extended on both sides of the road.

His sight can't capture all the disseminating spontaneity of the enthralling all-encompassing views. The car continued moving to the opposite direction of the town's airport into a calmer finely constructed quarters plainly depicting a residential area with superficially unfluctuating features of red bricks, iron stones, and tall standing walls. That was obviously one of the prominent features of the town's construction. Not much commotion in the area at that time of the hour, only few individuals with formal outfits, some walking and some on bicycles obviously returning from the town. They proceeded beside a hill, on top of which was a mosque with two mosaic pedestals. Beyond the hill, the pitch was an open ground with more palpable stretch of red soil and a podium standing at the gradient of the hill.

'This is freedom square, and on this side is the university of Bahr El Ghazal', *muqaddum* Tom said, pointing to the other side. There was a total silence at the mention of freedom square and a higher educational institution where a mark of history and the pursuit for the exercise of responsible independent judgement collided under the banner of war zone.

It was already six years into the rule of the regime in power in the country. The regime exercised every possible means to secure their governance with a firm presence in the country. Like every other town, the obvious sight of uniformed men roaming from random directions was a very familiar expectation. That was the glimpse of life in that phase in the country. His enlistment to the town was a verdict that was meant to realign him; he instead was provoked to prevail the odds. For he was indeed at the interval to entrusting the journey to a daring call.

They proceeded into a very sizeable residential area built with mostly rectangular constructions roofed with grey silver zincs sparsely spread amongst conical roofed thatched huts and densely branched trees, a slight disparity to the colonial-built designs on the previous suburbs. The drive was down and up a valley with imposing semblance. All in all, the people, the place, the combination of motions and constructed stasis were a revelation into the shape of the town as they passed through and beyond. Wau was the town.

They finally arrived at the residence on the opposite side at the fringe of the town. Anwar could not believe his eyes. The winter sun was dawning beyond the horizon, spreading golden beams over the graphic shapes of the distant settings. Right in front of him were very extensive buildings bulwarked from view by dense hardwood trees. The enclosure displayed classic colonial architecture: rectangular brick buildings, high roofs, and tall mahogany windows and doors. He presumed it to be a learning facility.

Like every Northerner who travels South for the first time, he was astonished. But that astonishment added to his sentiments a reason to persist on what had led him there. They entered the courtyard where they were greeted by a bunch of soldiers in their casual outfits, playing dominoes. These were his Northern compatriots with all their colours, random hugging and a strong slap on the palm of the hand followed by 'Hamdila ala salama'. 'Hamdila ala salama' was heard all over the place.

He could not remember all of them on that first day. However, few of them stood out. He recognised Lieutenant Colonel, *naqib* Taher Huzaifa, an upright rigid-figured man with the ordinary expression of a Northerner on his face. That was because he had showed him his place in a room they are going to share. The next person he had to distinguish was obviously Tom, his travelling companion. They have been together on the plane in this epic journey south of the country. Nonetheless, there was more of greetings between them as they arrived the intended destination in such a time in the history of the country.

'Hamdilla alla salama', said another very coarse voice.

From that instant, Anwar guessed him to be the resident chief officer, colonel, *aqid* Abdel Aziz Bilal. He was not fond of senior officers who were what moved him south of the country. This time he had to do the impossible not to escape the punishment but to pertain to his passion, to the call for what is more honourable to a soldier—his country. He stood and saluted him. The officer in chief, colonel Abdel Aziz, saluted back.

'Did you have a walk around the place?' he asked.

Shaking his head, Anwar replied, 'We just arrived, sir'.

'Come with me, allow me to take you for a tour', said the commander as he led the way for them strolling into the open veranda facing the town.

'This is a war zone. In any case, you are better off here than the walls of the prison', he said, tapping Anwar's shoulder with his right hand whilst they stood face-to-face with each other. Anwar nodded in regard for a man whom he unexpectedly begun to see a nerve that could stand for some kind of truth, kindness, and vigour.

Dinner was served in the late afternoon. Amusingly, those were the same rations he had been used to having in his previous locations. One of the major connection instruments in cultural assortments, he came to realise, was what people ate, notwithstanding the fact it intrigues association in spite of any geographic disparities. It was a condescending respite to that far-reaching journey. To Anwar, the North is brought into this new cantonment as something that presented him an absolution to consider his confinement as a blessing in disguise, a hiding that would eventually fragmentise and refute his fright and build his vigour level by level until that person with sanctioned passion to serve would rise to no retreat. In spite of what preceded, Anwar was gifted with impulsive bravery that helped him integrate exclusively wherever he goes. On that dinner table, though sitting inaudibly, he had already become one of the squadrons of the diversity of the North in the jungle of the South.

He entered into the building walking through a cold dark corridor that led towards the rooms of the wide-ranging residence; a vastly built infrastructure with many rooms and encompassing verandas, one of which he was going to share with the two field officials, *naqib* Taher and *muqaddam* Tom.

A lit lantern on the side table glowed and illuminated the dim shade of the night-time. He could smell the aroma of the kerosene disseminating in the air. Tom sat on his bedside, reciting the Holy Quran. He chose not to interpose his meditation and proceeded towards a bed beside a semi-crumpling window in a high-ceilinged room with zinc roof coned and exposed beyond logs of fine woods.

As he sat by the bed, gazing around the room, his mind redirected him to his arrival to reimagine himself sited aboard the plane and arriving to town. Since he had arrived his destination in the evidently significant journey, he pondered, what more could a man seek? He is a very fine lad with an unprejudiced sentiment. He could not forbear meeting the woman of his dreams. If mortality was the ultimatum in his journey, then all the endowments of a fulfilled life have to be authentically accomplished. Like every militant, Anwar was aware there persisted another fight as tough as the fight of the battlefield in a man's life—the fight for love, where a man lays down his conceits, self-absorption, and failures and forages for a soulmate as the eventual attainment of self-assertion. That was an obviously self-instigating make-believe to circumnavigate the faintness of the silent night.

THE FIRST PARADE

The dawn approached with composure in the quite outskirt of the town. It was downright, it was autumnal. Anwar could smell the scents of decayed barks ascending with the morning vapour from beneath the dense trees outside the building, disseminating through the fissures lining of the window beside him. Except for the decayed woody smell coming from the forest scents, the morning was as quiet as in the deserts. The only sounds he could hear was the wind whistling overhead beside the tall walls. For a while, Anwar was inaudibly seated, repositioning his consciousness to the fact he was no longer where the voice of the 'muazin' wakes the believers for prayers in the early dawn of the day; that could be heard, he presumed, somewhere in the town.

He sat by the bed for a while and placed beside his pillow a vintage Panasonic radio covered with a brown leather he had brought with him. He gazed around the room for his roommates in the opaque radiance of the dawn; they were all slumbered in their beds. The radio had an eloquent pulse in the quietness of the morning. Those sound waves brought along numerous updates from around the world into his confinement. For a while, he felt himself again, unaltered with the disappointment of his sanctioning. His unwavering character had reclaimed the inner liberty to delving into the unknown. From those preliminary impressions, he was drawn to imagine there must be much to the town than just the confinement of his residence.

Still sitting on the bedside, the sound of the wind insistently rustling the overhanging trees appeased his peripatetic mind, and he started to doze off again, laid his head on the pillow, and began snoring right away. His imaginations soared the wild and vast distances whilst the radio was on, randomly narrating on worlds so far away from his.

In a snitch of time, he woke from sleep again, got up from the bed walking blurrily to a pile of tin boxes, over which he had put his hand luggage. As he picked his towel and toothbrush, Tom came walking in. 'Sabah el khier'.

He said drying his hair with his towel. 'We start late here because the mornings are uncertain. You got to rush to that burel', he said, pointing through the window to a detached building of the lavatory, beside which was set the bathing water.

Anwar looked at him.

'Go', he said. 'This is how things work here. Just make your way. The tea is being served, and the whistle will soon go'.

He looked at him astonished at his reproach and walked out of the building to the freshness of the early hour of the morning. The quietness was so appealing, except for sounds of the random motions in their hostel. He could observe with a settled composure all the surrounding locations adjacent to their camp with only few houses far-flung between dense mango trees. The walls around bore stains of war, an obvious indication of previous battleground and, thus, could have been a precarious location for many. The wind was slow-moving, gentle, and cold. He was wearing a thin *jalabia*, a popular Northern outfit, and was feeling the chills of the different weather.

He walked to the water burels, found a bowl inside it and some small jerrycans. He pulled up his sleeve, picked a jerrycan, walked a step into the wet grounds of the doorway.

'How has our country treated you?' he heard someone talk as the water was being poured into a jerrycan. That was *naqib* Maher Akram, a very young military officer with the rank of Captain slender-looking figure with a very civilised outlook. He had a darker skin tone. Anwar realised meeting him on his arrival the day before. He was amongst the bunch but rather kept a vigilant gaze around the place with wide hazel eyes. He was the least talkative but instead was quite sharp-eyed.

'Good so far, let's see what is going to come', Anwar replied.

'This is how things are here, this is the lavatory', he said. Pointing to the build, he added, 'That's the kitchen and tea place. You know your bedroom, simply start getting used to things like that'.

'That's normal for me, my brother. I have already begun to see that. Besides, it's a beautiful countryside'.

'It is, but so much is concealed by that beauty. Some days are quite harsh', Maher replied, scratching his hair. He had been in the camp for three good years. He was sent to the front line once. The experience left a lasting psychological ripple on his tenderfoot start on one desolate battleground. He had to stay in the camp for a good number of months to recaption his sanity.

'God reward you with goodness, my brother', Anwar said, looking at Maher.

They strolled quietly to a thatched shed adjacent to a window that opened from the kitchen, where the tea was being served every day. Maher's shy persona didn't permit him to indulge into much conversation with Anwar who decided not to be very interrogative himself. They got to the spot crammed with fellow army men. He took his cup of tea and hurried to the room to get dressed up. Putting on a densely pouched khaki uniform, heavy boots, and a face cap, Anwar dressed like a soldier going into combat.

With the sound of the whistle blowing tirelessly into the all-embracing empyrean, he marched into the terrace. They gathered for the morning parade on a spacious arena encompassed by tall standing rectangular buildings, a space that would certainly have been where students assembled when the building was used for its purpose. The area had the tranquillity of a countryside muteness. Where he stood in attention, the only sound awakening the surrounding was the whistling reverberation. The parade commenced with them marching forward and backwards at the sounds of the whistle and commands of the director. Red dust shrouded their surrounding in the intensity of the morning sunshine. The trainer doesn't converse; he screams all the time as much as he never ran out of tone. He knew well he had to put up with all these by applying his instincts to scale, which approach should be appropriate. For that is a jungle of lonesome men in a squad.

'First Sergeant Anwar Fareed'.

His presence was announced by the commander as a new internee who had joined the camp. His heart began to pound loudly; he was sure he could hear it. He marched right foot forward and left foot adjacent to salute and say his name and his battalion. There was a stillness, not in the mass, in his consciousness as that of an instant of rebirth. He was at that point, one of the masses in the morning training with his squad under the heat of the winter sun. Not sure whether it was himself alone, he began to feel the awkward sensation of a hollow empty stomach. He can't just dash that feeling to the excitement of getting started. He felt his essence perverting with indispensable commitment to the patriot cause. It was an introspective experience, for he was indeed a captive patriot from the North freed to a martial call. He marched in the shrouded red dust.

'First Sergeant Anwar FadlAllah Fareed, Third Infantry Division', he replied with the loudest possible voice. As he stepped back to his place on the line, he postured with a liberated stamina, for he had come to carry a duty so demanding of his vigour.

They continued marching in ceaseless motions. The first parade of the day was the focal procession. He could see more officials he hadn't met on his arrival. Everybody attended with reverence. The dust continued to shroud. As he inhaled, he could smell the undertones of mud dredged from the ground by the combat boots.

He walked from the parade ground to the build promenading towards a lone path that led to an extension of the building's entryway. The structure is attached to the building in an L silhouette and enclosed with low stone-built wall and columns of screened windows. An African tulip tree stood right at the side of the entrance. The branches had grown baren with the turn of the season. The winter winds have shaken the tiny leaves off the petioles, leaving behind a bronze sculpt of branches. The morning sunrays hurled into the veranda with a golden facade. He walked into the building to his room to figure out how the rest of the day would look like. His batches were shuffling around the building, some chewing snacks and carrying a cup of tea, whilst some of them happened to be on a persistent routine of not staying in one location.

Their conversations were perpetual, around almost a single incidence over and over. It was obvious most of them pride themselves for being in the army. The compound was shrouded in such a way they could observe that side of the town without being seen. That buffered zone gave them the freedom to mingle within the compound in casual outfits, sandals, and even bare chest.

On the second day of his arrival in town, he was awakened by an early morning unyielding wintry breeze. That morning had a different tone with a sudden ascending sound of what he recognised as the cattle egret birds vacated their sleep precincts on the trees. Their reverberations gratified the dawning day with rhythms of loud rickrack, something he hasn't realised from the previous day. Or maybe he had consciously begun to attend to the new location, adopting to the sensory draws which can provoke him to ponder how the day ahead would be spent. The wind gasped in intermitted blows against the study walls, carrying the rickrack calls of the hovering birds. That was a morning with sheer disengagement of any fear from the ecosystem.

He got off his bed, walked out of the room through the front porch to where the janitor was preparing the fireplace for the morning tea. His name was *mulazim* Hamid Pasha, a soldier and the steward in the complex. Hamid was a tall slender grey-haired man in his late fifties. He wore an oversized light-shaded suede army uniform and pairs of sandals. From the looks, he was not the kind person that talks much.

Anwar found him inside the shabbily built thatched shed, where he couldn't stand under in full height because his stature overextended the roof. Placed on a table next to him was some consignments of sugar in a steel plate, an orange plastic cup filled with tea leaves, and a smaller cup with mixed spices. A bundle of bread was put on an empty woven jute sack on the ground beside the table. Anwar looked at him from the door of the shed and nodded, saying, 'Sabah el khier?'

'Sabah el noor', he responded. 'The tea will be ready soon, *janabu*'.

The whistle was blown as many times as possible, high-pitched into the stillness of the morning. They began marching as energetically as possible. The dust shrouded soaring into the air and disseminating earth like smells. Their resident commander walked to the front with some statements, and they were disseminated for the day.

He spent his whole day in observation of who could be his guidance to know the town. Though a detainee, that, to him, was a subject to a limited time. For what he intended to be to manifest itself, he had to reach beyond the shelter of that quarantine.

Contrary to his speculations, the circumstances in the setup were not that strict as they were in the training camps. Their routine included waking up at 5:00 a.m. and getting ready for the day. Then teatime was around 6:00 a.m. Their morning parade was at 7:00 a.m. They conduct the first parade when the sun had already risen. After that, they are dispersed to the tasks of the day. They get involved in all the features of the daily routine. That included cleaning the compound, filling the water tups, and preparing the meals. Above all, they had to be vigilant of any people going about their routines to their fields or entering the town from that direction. They take rounds in patrolling their area. Also being a backup base, specifically for military exchange of the frontline combatants, there was not much to be done during the day, except for keeping watch. They exchanged on intervals. So those remaining in the base were meant to guard the town and remain in standby.

The day passed. Whereas Anwar went and stood inside the building beside the doorway, watching the town features fade in faintness of the night-time. Night-time had approached. He could not set his mind off what his path was leading to. Hidden beneath the splendour of the sky above was the concealed mystery of his call of duty. As his military training pertains, losing his soul for this cause would be an absolute bravery. Yet for Anwar, the clench to life is a tougher grip. He did not come to perish in the unknown wild. He came to seek vindication to the intrusive order of the ruling structure in leading the country to war, to redefine his disposition and construct a more uncompromising version of his views to resisting the disparities in the socio-political spectrum of his country. Was military service the permitted course in a case that substantial as life itself? He sighed.

On the third day of his arrival, he walked up efficiently as he had begun to get accustomed to his new home and adopting to the conditions of the cantonment; a very quiet morning with a happy anticipation of a new adventure in a duty that drew him wholly.

'Sabah el khier', he said.

'Sabah el noor', Hamid responded, pouring gasoline from a stained brown jerrycan onto some mounds of charcoal on an oven. He pulled a matchbox from his pocket and flashed the matchstick on the charcoal. Unknowingly, some of the charcoals were sparkly. Meanwhile, he walked out of the shed to fetch some water in a large silver bowl, with which he would prepare the morning tea. Whilst talking to Anwar, a sharp wind blew, and a sparkly blaze flew to the thatched wall. When he was pouring the fuel, some splintered onto the grass wall of the shed, so it caught fire. They first glanced at each other at the unexpected view of what was going on. Then with a sudden rapture, they screamed, 'Hareeeg, hareeeg!' which means 'Fire, fire!'

Both rushed to where the barrels were lined, and with larger buckets, they carried the water and poured it on the burning shed. Not everyone seemed to be awake yet. And in the dry winter days, the shed had slight dampness, so it became unlikely to put off the flames. They stood watching the assembled grass crumpling in fragments of ashes. In a matter of minutes, a structure of black standing timbers replaced the scene. After all, it was shabbily built.

Going to the parade, he felt indistinct from the unexpected happenings of the morning. Unlike his morning wake-up, he began to feel his physique was being predisposed to depreciate from the overwhelm. When the assembly was over, they dispersed to the day's activities. Only for him, he had to report to the main garrison headquarters in the region. He was anticipating with keen curiosity how he would meet their chief commander, the *Liwa* in the region. *Liwa* Abdel Azeem Andal was his name as he was told. He resides in the main barrack adjacent to the town's airport. He wondered if what was reported of him would influence the chief commander. That encounter would set the grounds for his path in that side of the country and perhaps the entire course of his military career.

OUT OF THE ORDINARY

I t was a morning that was so disquieted after the incident of the previous day. Anwar woke as early as he could. The only other person awake was *mulazim* Hamid, taking the role of a janitor. He realised Hamid was the do-it-all superintendent soldier when it comes to the domestic works. He, of course, could not learn much from him about the town's army commander-in-chief. So he just walked to him to have a normal conversation.

'Sabah el khier?' Anwar started.

'Sabah el noor', Hamid responded as cool as he could be, even with no shade, where he could carry his duties with ease.

Whilst everybody was engrossed in their routine assignments that morning, Anwar and Tom, accompanied by *mulazim* Hamid and some of the officer cadets, took off to the headquarters of the army garrison, a place called Grinty. Grinty lay on the other side of the airport north of the town, which meant their drive would take the reverse route of his arrival. In a while, the sights had obscured his thoughts from any speculations of how he would meet the commanders at the main garrison. He began to feel tentative of who he was going to meet. Seated on the back of the military vehicle with two of the military cadets beside him and *naqib* Maher, he realised how reticent they were in the journey. Trying to converse in the silence, he cleared his throat. 'Who is the commander I would meet?' he asked his colleagues.

'You won't meet him. You will only meet the storekeeper'. It was Maher, his new colleague.

'Hey, we better not meet him. He is very furious-tempered and aggressive in tone. He is quite busy too'. That was Hamid who was going to collect rations for their pantry.

His apprehension escalated. He could feel his adrenaline rushing through his blood. He wondered whether their responses were deliberate objections or warnings.

'We are going to meet the store person only, and we will be returning', his colleague continued.

Feeling the need to understand what could possibly go wrong, he asked, 'How are things with him then?'

'You mean the chief commander? He is pretty tough. You just have to obey him when you meet him'.

To Anwar, the early morning drive was filled with utter self-composure. Again, travelling on the inverse of the same road that landed him to his base the day he arrived, one side extended to an obviously bureaucratic constructions with uniformed paths. The streets were quiet and foggy. Rusts on the zincs displayed from amongst sluggish trees as they drove closer to town. The other direction had more traditional constructions extending beyond blocks and blocks of seemingly endless buildings, shades, and shrubs. The corridor of their ride had factually partitioned the town into uncoherent societal lines. It ingrained a timeline of the town's edifices.

Again, passing the roundabout and the narrow bridge, the morning vapour smells grassy. They entered the marketplace. In that hour of the morning, it was lined up with vendors selling tea in one point, and nearby were jerrycans of petrol besides piles of car tyres.

They entered a compound of tall standing dark green-painted constructions. The place serves as the headquarters, the armoury, and a cantonment. He could barely distinguish the buildings from the trees as the colours were uniformly laid across the compound. Clusters of huts stood at the distant end of the complex. All around were random groups of men in different sorts of uniforms. A group of the cadets were undergoing training on one side. He paid close attention to some batch jogging by and singing artillery songs.

He wanted to capture what the words were, for a while zooming in his attention to the lyrics. Their vehicle began to move in a ridiculously slow pace even so, they could not catch with the jogging internees. He looked at his friends to say something, only to see from behind where the joggers had passed, two men in uniform rustling. One on the top was punching so hard, and no one seemed to be doing anything about that. He jumped off the back of the wandering Toyota, ran to the site of the fight, and with a strong grip, pulled the man on the top, clenching his arms at the elbow on his chest. The combatant pulled himself off Anwar, stretched his shoulder, and turned around to face Anwar.

'This is wrong, not right!' Anwar yelled at them.

'Are you the officer First Sergeant Anwar FadlAllah?' he asked, looking at Anwar.

It was only then that he realised the batch on the pocket of his shirt; he was the brigadier general, popularly called *Liwa* Abdel Azeem around the town. Anwar quickly pulled himself with legs firmly adjacent to each other in an objecting attention, raised his hand in a one-count movement of a salute. 'Yes, sir', he responded.

Liwa Abdel Azeem leaned forward so close to Anwar's face that he could smell the vapour from his breath. It was a strong insolent and harsh smell of a cigar. With a course voice, he said, 'Don't you ever interfere'. He straightened his shoulders and walked off.

Anwar had never felt his heart pound this much. He could even hear the sound. There is nothing he could do to defend, even explain, his reaction. He was left alone standing in the heat of the winter sun. Neither the commander nor the subordinate soldier was there on their rustling ground; they disappeared amongst rows of tents, shelters, and barracks lining up the army village.

There, Anwar was standing still. What an awkward encounter. How different could things have been? What he cannot dispute was what happened had set him off, and yeah, thanks to his spontaneous drive to action. His was not interference; it was an instantaneous altruistic response to a situation with a tendency to an authoritarian to a rule deficient of sympathy.

'You missed an instant of a very intense rage. We could all have been detained due to your over reaction'. That was Tom, one of his companions, talking. 'Now let's hurry to the store and get back to our side of freedom'.

'You just missed a punch, my friend'. That was Maher talking, trying to make a fun of the situation.

'Sure', Anwar replied with a sigh, carrying his body off the spot in a march of surrender. Their car was parked by the side of the incident. He could feel his body almost trembling; they strolled to a section of warehouses vertically positioned on one side of the military multipart. What was so astonishing was everyone disappeared; it was the three of them on the path to the warehouse.

'What did he say?' Tom asked.

'Not to interfere', Anwar answered.

'Anwar!' the storekeeper shouted from behind his counter from the distance as they approached.

'Yes, sir', Anwar responded with a sense of regained sanity and coming back to a conscious reality. He felt his sentiments entangled as he approached the storekeeper who greeted him with a strong handshake, even though they were meeting for the first time.

'I am very flexible here. Just watch your actions, and you will do your job well'. *naqib* Santino, as he was popularly known amongst the military personnel, was the officer in charge of the granaries and all the necessities of the officers and cadets.

He picked his allocated luggage, leaned on the table with the backpack hanging on the side of his shoulder, and signed the paper document. Certainly, none of them was staying any longer. They have just set off to an unusual start. They wanted to take off hurriedly, lest the get delayed by another provocative encounter.

'Anwar', the storekeeper *naqib* Santino Fodul called out again with the same loud tone. This time he walked out from behind his counter, tapped Anwar on the shoulder, and whispered into his face, 'I am here if you need anything'. Anwar shook his hand, nodding in a sigh to relief his worry.

He felt reassured after meeting the storekeeper *naqib* Santino, a Southern man, with no obvious tribal signs on the face. Or rather a man of no tribe because his accent was more of a Northerner. All these details were irrelevant; what was substantial at that instant was him finding a judicious confidant in a cause evinced in the livelihoods of the disadvantaged of the society.

They returned to their residence from a day out of the ordinary with a mixed sense of reassurance and a weight in the chest. What would have happened if his instincts did not prompt him to an instantaneous response? Whilst the encounter was unusual, the approach of the storekeeper had signalled to him a reinforcement of his instinct. What could he have imagined in this apprehending disposition in the process of getting to have a place in the town? Well, that would have been a plain journey of picking military compendium and a ride back to his base town, something which his hankering capacity wouldn't settle for, a simple ride. He pondered how the sequences and escalation of the incidences that occurred in just few days of his arrival were adequately provocative to the situation of a detainee.

So not to spend more time in the flashes of the detestation of the day, he walked out of his room into the veranda, looking for *naqib* Maher. He walked out of the room into the veranda with an open window sealed with transparent aluminium shield. He could see Maher with folded legs against a tree, sitting stress-free besides a bunch of colleagues playing dominoes in the compound.

He went beside him, pulled a chair, and asked Maher quietly, looking at him, 'Do you know any of the locals in town?' Maher was a bit astounded. Usually, when any disappointing event happened in the residence, the soldiers don't speak of it.

To clarify, he thought of asking again. 'What do you mean?' he asked.

'I mean individuals, families', he said.

Maher was an aloof stay-at-home resident for most of the time before Anwar arrived, though he knew few people. He thought it was too early for Anwar to get into meeting anyone.

'You go and finish your resting', Maher said. He thought the only thing troubling Anwar was the burnt cookhouse. 'Don't worry about the cookhouse, it will be rebuilt soon'.

Taking the advice, Anwar went inside the building for his resting. He picked his radio, turned it on, and laid himself on the bed to begin a nap, only to hear his name being called again.

'Ya, Anwar', his new friend Maher called him out after they had only a few minutes of resting. Maher might have realised that he had become Anwar's last resort in his estrangement. Or he might be a little off in his mind to be out of etiquette.

Still with his uniform, he walked out of the room to the porch, looked at Maher, and responded with a lazy tone, 'What's wrong with you calling me out like that?'

'You burnt the cookhouse, that is what's wrong', Maher said, laughing. Anwar was quiet. 'Aaah, I am joking, believe me', Maher continued. Again, no response. 'But how can you just stand there and watch the shed collapse in fire? You can't put off a small flame as that?' he said mockingly.

'Let me go and make some tea', Anwar responded

Besides the rumples of the burnt shed was the actual kitchen in the main building. He entered the kitchen, a place that was so condensed with all the cooking equipment placed disorderly. Hamid was preparing the late-night meal for the day. He walked around the kitchen in search of a sizeable cup to drench his wearying thoughts in the aroma of a delectable cup of tea.

'Hey, Anwar', Maher called out again and came to the door of the crowed kitchen.

'Let's go out to have some tea from a woman's hand. They put the ingredients in proper measures, you know', Maher said, jokingly. He paused, looking at Anwar who had enough to venture for the day. Yet besides that, he had to deal with Maher's arrogant jokes. He reached out for a plastic orange cup on a shabby iron shelf that was obviously a canteen shelve. Maher realised his jokes weren't helping, so he entered the tiny kitchenette and said to Anwar with a more solemn tenor, 'Don't be that hard on yourself, my friend. Take things easy'. And he walked off.

Anwar picked a smoke-stained casserole that he had put on the oven and filled his cup with the boiled ingredients. It had taken overtime, and the stock had boiled strenuously. As a result, the tea turned pungent from the fumes of the casserole. He took a sip from the plastic mug. He couldn't distinguish the savour of the long-awaited drink. He had only burnt his tongue. Feeling the disgust, he put the cup on the floorboard of the only window in the kitchenette and walked out.

In that instant, he thought the best idea was to take a walk in the suburb like Maher suggested. Maybe fate would bring around something good to release his apprehension. He walked to his location and with a rather reserved tone, said, 'Let's go to where you suggested'.

Maher looked at him and smiled. He didn't seem offended anymore. He had enough of distress to not be trapped in any offensive condition. He had learnt that the hard way.

'This was what I suggested. How did your tea go?'

'Not so good', Anwar replied.

'You were using the casserole for boiling fresh milk. You can't make a plain tea in that. It would come pungent because it is not meant for plain tea. It is a milk casserole'.

'Why all this explanation over a casserole? I got it already!' Anwar exclaimed.

'This is how the talks go around here. Not much serious stuff', Maher responded with an agitated gesture.

They walked out of their compound silently as if in escape. Maher took a different direction from what Anwar presumed they were going to take.

'This way', Maher summoned with a hand gesture, seeing that Anwar was going to take the usual route. Anwar followed to a slender path that slid from the hill to the main wide road. They walked between dozens of cows, returning to town from a grazing ground.

'There is a low land down this path', Maher said. He had to shout as the cows were mooing all over the area. The road smell like a mowed lawn with an undertone odour of dust towering from the treaded ground. Several of them bore twisted horns stretching sideway, and they moved with indolent strolls along the path.

'Why are we not taking the main route from the compound?' Anwar asked.

Maher moved a step towards him. 'We had enough trouble for today, haa. This route will take us there as well'.

Anwar realised how the magnitude of his impulsiveness could be retrospective at some point. He now needed more caution in any of his actions. However, he understood very well that it was not himself alone faced with troubled consequences. Sneaking between the herds, they crossed the wide street to the other side into a cluster of slender-spaced huts, shanty-thatched sheds, and concise footpaths—an obvious deserted area. He was tempted to ask where the residents are, but he decided to caution himself to leave the question for another time.

'Does this path take us to the place?' Anwar asked as he followed Maher along the path.

'Let me show you how people live here, my friend. Trust me, we will get there', Maher responded.

'Okay. Then when are we getting there?' Anwar asked.

'Not far', Maher said as they reached the edge of a wider path that diverged from the main road.

To their left, they watched the resplendence of the domestic bovine strolling the streets beneath sunbeams in the rising dust, whilst they took a concealed accessory pathway. The suburb is called Nazareth, an extended construction of the town just right at the edge with only few buildings in the vicinity with similar big assemblies of stone and brick-built walls.

A distance away from where they found the grass thatches was Uncle Khamis's place in a neighbouring suburb called Gonia. Uncle Khamis and his family were a family that Maher got to connect with when he begun his duty in Wau. He could see their barracks concealed in the distance by the hardwood trees over the hill.

'Salam aleikum', Maher said as they stood at the ingress of a yard far spreading into a couple of plots. The gate was a double-bamboo-constructed edifice. They entered a fence magnifically assembled with poles of bamboo and interweaved thatches. The house was a high build with a zinc rooftop, a characteristic feature of the buildings in town. The shiny grey zinc was predominant in all directions, with rustic stains depicting the differences between the older and the newly built buildings.

They found a man wearing a galabia sitting on a wooden chair similar to what they have in their camp. That was Uncle Khamis, the owner of the house. After being seated where the view was a perpetual spectrum of dense vegetation and shelters, they began a very unrevealing conversation. Maher introduced his new colleague to Khamis. The family has been supportive to him in his solitary over the years of feeling the pressure of military life. Maher thought Anwar would need such a solace from the time his candour attitude had set him forth.

Anwar was informed that conflicts erupted frequently, with clashes arising from ethnic frictions. Most of the discrepancies were induced by unequal involvement in local decision-makings. Most leaders were promptly tempted to tribal affiliations. More than a decade after the second civil war, he found out that the suburb had inclined to receiving civilians from the surrounding areas. By the winter of that year, the season of his arrival, the town was already pledged with rising vicious conflicts. Maher turned out not be the psychopath he suspected. In the desire to end the war, the men create self-justifying mechanisms. Maher's was being delusional. He was the link to forming an impetus to a revolution. Like Maher, the soldier beaten that day was planning to sneak ammunitions to some fragments of armed groups in town.

'So this is our town. How is the reality treating you?' Uncle Khamis asked, looking at Anwar.

'Like a military life would do', Anwar responded. 'Since arriving, it has been a strict compact schedule'.

'What would you say coming to Wau has added to your military career?' Khamis asked.

'I see Sudan in a different way. I question my judgements in being in the military. I have seen the cost of war in the last two days', he said.

'We have to admit that those inside are also part of the struggle in the revolution', Khamis said. They were all silent at Khamis's response. They realised that they were Northern army men, and Uncle Khamis the characterised the silent observer whose views cannot be discounted. Yet in their excavation of the substances of the conflicts, there remained many shared sentiments for all the detriments so confounding to console. Anwar felt his temperature rise. His body started to agitate. The dive of their conversation had taken a path of unfathomable penetration of the cause into his being.

Their silence was interrupted by people entering the house—children. Their entrance being far from where the guests were sitting allowed them to proceed on their way, running to the main building. Khamis's wife entered and walked towards the guests to greet them. Another girl followed afterwards, entering, running through the gate. Her legs were shrouded with dust. She wore green sandals, a round skirt, and her hair was plaited prettily. He didn't get to see the face. Watching the children run into the house, Anwar felt the refinements of beauty, cosiness, and calm about Khamis's place. Watching his friend Maher gestured with his head for them to start going, they had to leave to allow Khamis to attend to his family.

'You have to make another visit for a banquet with our new friend Anwar', Khamis said to Maher.

'Happy to meet you, Uncle Khamis', Anwar responded.

'Are you getting used to walking the distance?' Khamis asked as they were leaving the house.

'Soon he will', Maher answered.

They reached their residence in no time. Maher had already got Anwar trained in a long-distance walk. That visit remained for them a twilight of reminiscence.

THE MALARIA OF THE SOUTH

T he malaria of the South was a tale of the power of a parasite in the persistent disentanglement of human sanity and intuition. As much as he had heard of the stories of people being sick with the malaria, he had never experienced the magnitude of what that felt like—until he travelled to the South, and that time came. Food in the camp became completely abhorrent. He grew frail over one day. They drove him to the military hospital in town. When they arrived at the hospital, he was already looking very blurry and nauseous. Though the hospital was instigated with so much to observe, in that instance, for Anwar, there was no lure to curious observations that day. He only had his medical investigations then his medications and returned to his residence.

Cold breezes disguised the following days and nights in a successive way. The season had totally perverted for him. Lying in bed, his mind soared to the time of his arrival aboard the Lockheed L-100-20 Hercules. Tears were burning his eyes. He turned his frailer feverish body to the side and felt a warm tear running to his ears, a journey so delineating to his career and life. His mind began to beseech his weary soul with inexplicable questions.

Can he doubt his intuition?

Could he possibly be anything in this remotely uncertain part of the country?

Should he thrust onto the subtility of his aspirations?

Why should he come all this way? Why shouldn't he?

Now that he reached, he beseeched that the time he spent in the town could compliment his journey.

That radio he carried all the way from the North remained his all-time companion. With it, he connected to a world different from his confinement: a world of news broadcast and people who make decisions on the behalf of others; a world of sports where the names of the two popular sport teams in the country, Hilal and Marekh, sieged the sports broadcasting. There was also the world of music. He loved tuning into that different world that indulged his intuitions into subtle urges to a conviction that the imagined could potentially be a remanence to an anticipated outcome. The radio, to him, conveys voices that spoke into his subconscious, voices that would ignite his passion; and where he found no endorsement for his compelling ideas, those voices became sources of reinforcement and at times reproof. He carried it wherever he is posted.

The sound of the radio become an indication of his presence in the residence. It was placed constantly next to his pillow. Lying in his sickness, he would just stretch over, press the power button, and tune to the news; something he did day after day to follow any peace talks taking place. Anywhere he had travelled up to that time, the public discourses just converged to the shared theme: peace. He too was living in anticipation of that peace. He had longed to see his call of duty hold a higher purpose wherever he is stationed.

His colleagues Maher, Tom, and Taher provided some time of extensive conversation that should otherwise deviate his sensitivity from the malaria. Yet that was not enough. For there was a heavy yank in his heart. The fragility was like a call for a sentimental demand to that which would complete him. Over his journey, he had felt fractional in a story so profound and complete. The malaise had urged his emotion to seek an attending ear and a compatriot to a cautious route towards a viable feat.

His thoughts persisted to wonder who that girl he saw at Khamis's place could be. For him, it sounds contemptable to ask anyone, not even Maher. For once, he found a pursuit that had the particulars of a personal yet a far-reaching significance. Was it the malaria deluding him from reality, or was he just too affected by emotional inadequacies? His sentiments baffled at the thought. His devotion to his radio had not been sufficient to elude the queasiness of the malaria.

After spending a whole week in sick bed, Anwar knew he had to make for himself a sound refuge in town. The only place in mind was Uncle Khamis's place. He pulled himself out of the bed, put on a casual outfit and walked out of the room to the compound. He walked to the bare outlet of the veranda, searching who amongst his colleagues would be around the compound. Everybody seemed to be either on the other side of the compound or even busy lingering in town. He strolled to where Maher took them to a path to Khamis's house. Again, no one was in sight. He started moving towards the crossing ground where they met the herds.

The street was empty. He had not been out of his room for most of the week. From his position, the evening sun portrayed a colour of a whole new world right in his sight. He felt a refreshing breeze, like he never has never been enchanted this much since arriving his confinement. He crossed hastily to the side of the clumsily aggregated huts. Trailing through the narrow passageways between the huts, he came across a street vendor selling sugar cane on a wheelbarrow. 'How much?' he asked in a haste. He thought that would be a good thing to bring along. The canes were sprouted tall poles that the merchant had to cut them at the internodes to make it possible to carry.

Carrying the bundle of the cane stalks on one hand, he walked to where he believed was the house. He pushed the door open with the other hand. So not to stand knocking and risk being seen, he entered pulling in the sugar cane sticks through the door.

'Salam aleikum?' he said, standing by the gate. Nobody seemed to be around the vicinity of his arrival. So quite was the place. The breeze was dry and cold. The golden afternoon sun shone bright over the fence on the creased brick wall of the house, convening a warmth around the build. In the stillness, he beheld a small rectangular chamber on the wall where an open window was shielded with grey iron shield. He can't see through as it was positioned high, almost close to the roof like an attic. Near what he presumed as the front porch was a flower garden with diminutive winter plants in fantastic display. At that time of the season, the leaves had turned pale yellow. Flowered foliage dropped on the ground beside the standing pedestals. All were left drenched in the parched drift of the evening gale.

What should he do, he pondered. Since he had made this risky gesture, it would be better to ensue what would please his yearnings. So he walked towards the front porch. 'Salam aliekum', he called again.

'Aliekum el salam', Sarah said, sprinting out of one of the rooms towards the veranda. She wore a long oversized mauve purple robe, so long, so much that she had to clutch one side with her hand so as not to fall whilst walking. Her hair chanted like a fuzzy afro combo. She was as raw as a papaya tree. She provoked in him a prevailing innocence that reminded him of the palms of the desert, of home so far away. 'Aliekum el salam', she said again in a very understandable accent.

'I am Anwar', he responded.

'You were here the other day', she responded. 'Welcome', she continued. Though she did not go to where they were seated in the first visit, Sarah saw them through the window the time they were leaving, when they walked past the building.

'Here, I found this', he said, holding out the bundle of cane stalks to Sarah. 'I thought you might like it'.

He walked towards a few plastic-woven steel chairs lined by the wall of the narrow veranda. The open porch was facing a cylindrical flower garden by the wall. He could see dried veiling creepers on the rods holding the crest of the roof. The pale leafless stems spread a resinous, astringent, lemongrass-like smell. The ambience, though strong, was refreshing to his sensation. Sarah brought tea and a jug of water together with the sugar cane stalks. She was not apprehensive to pick one, peel off the cover, and munch the syrup out of the fibrous cane. Everybody at home had a share of the delectable snack. It was a product of home and one of the season's popular harvests.

'So what brought you to town?' Sarah asked, realising Anwar's calmness as she indulges in devouring the syrup out of the cane stalk.

'I am a military man', Anwar replied.

'I can see that you are', Sarah said, looking at Anwar. 'Why Wau?' she asked with a relatively assertive tone. Sarah had a blunt natural persona. Though he couldn't tell what she felt towards him, she portrayed knowledge and charm. She had familiarity to most of the accounts of the war. She must be a curious heeder to the tales of the events in the country, he guessed. She was the kind of person he would love to meet again and again. There was a daring connection, unexplained resemblance in the acumens and narration of their notions of cost of war.

'Would you say that the South would go?' Anwar asked, looking at Sarah.

'What if it did?' Sarah responded.

'You know what, young girl?' Anwar replied, noticing Sarah's persistent stances, 'They will only change the thatched fences, and you and I will have another talk then'.

All these times, they were sitting on the front porch, chewing the sugar cane, and zealously talking public matters. The sun had gone beyond the mounting trees, and a swarm of mosquito with fresh appetites started to appear in their gathering. It was already late in the evening, and Anwar was preparing to leave. That was meant to be a very short visit, and it turned out to be a self-enlightenment venture. He began to speculate what would be going on in the camp in his absence. So he got up to leave.

'I have to go, Sarah', he said and took off to the door.

Opening the door, the person in front of him getting off his bike was Uncle Khamis, arriving when it was almost dark.

'Oh, Anwar', he said, carrying the bicycle on one side over the elevated entrance at the gateway. 'You are leaving?'

'It is getting dark already', he said joking.

'I never met a soldier leaving a place because it is dark. I learnt that you had the malaria, it must have taken its toll off you?' he said.

He parked the bicycle by the house and invited Anwar for a dinner. Feeling the awkwardness of the situation, Anwar decided to accept the invitation. They walked into the house from the porch, where Sarah and Anwar had been eating the sugar cane. The untidy ground looked pale and grumpy with the scattered cane cellulite. Khamis had to invite him to a neater place. He was also embarrassed by the reception.

The house was a classic middle-class revelation of the town's supplies. The furniture set in the sitting room was a provincial set made from teak of the region and arranged in a very decent style in the room. A large bay window formed a curve that opened into the yard on the side of the house they had been accommodated on their first visit. An aluminium screen wire on a bay window allowed some fresh air in. The escape turned out to be a venture of a lifetime. There standing by the bay, he felt he belonged to the journey that brought him this far. He belonged to the cause and the utmost aspiration that was home.

'Do you drink, Anwar?' Khamis asked as he walked in finding Anwar standing by the window. He was quiet. 'Do you smoke then?' He nodded.

Khamis passed him a box of Bringi cigarettes he had in the palm of his hand. He realised Uncle Khamis was such a down-to-earth soul. He could be somebody to count on. Anwar picked one and put it between his lips and said, 'I was a part of a few members of an underground movement before I joined the army'.

They were standing quietly as this subject was risky in any discourse. But Anwar continued talking. 'I had realised a civil movement alone would not create a strong stimulus. There was a need to act from within, to be part of the rationale, to understand how a revolution could work . . .' With a deep sigh, he continued, 'Since it was a military regime in power'.

'How did you end up in the Southern divisions?' Khamis asked him.

'I was supposed to be in the prison', he said, looking at Khamis, then continued, 'I guess God thought the prison walls would be too trivial for a genius calling'.

'There is something more to the person that I see', Khamis responded light-heartedly.

He found Uncle Khamis to be very welcoming. He was open-minded as any Northern elder he would meet from where he came from. After all, he was one of the elite teachers in the town, educated in one of the esteemed educational institutes in the North called Bakht el Rida. Around this man's area were bundles of books, chalks, and several academic resources. That opened to him another window to what Sudan was. The more he got immersed in people's lives, the more the struggles overpower becomes insignificant. The challenge becomes knowing the country as it is.

They sat on a sitting area set with teak-framed couches Whilst they were seated, Sarah came in with a lit lamp and a tiny stove burning herbal incense to drive away mosquitoes.

'Can you bring the dinner, please? The man has already caught the malaria. Mosquitos are not problems anymore', he said to Sarah.

She left to the kitchen and returned with a dinner tray covered in an elegantly woven bucket. It was a dinner of dried fish dish and stiff porridge. It had similarity in taste to what he would find in many parts of the country where he had been before. The cuisine as well was an edifying reminder on the cultural assortments of the country. He got to meet Khamis's wife Matilda before leaving. She had a calm persona and wears a *thob* like a Northern woman.

He didn't meet Sarah on his way out. He thought it would be more awkward to call for her from the very start and the family clearly very conserved. He began to ponder, should he maintain his distance or take the risk of taking with her?

He made his way to the garrison in the stillness of the night. Like Uncle Khamis had said, soldiers don't get scared of the dark. The night was as dark as it could possibly be. He could only see few inches into the distance, except few faint sparkles of lights beyond some compounds. The divergence between the earth below and the heavens beyond the horizon was persuasively captivating in the vagueness of a sky filled with scattered twinkling stars. The wind panted in whirling sounds besides his ear as he marched steadily beside the road.

Totally detached from the town's suburbs was their barracks. There was always a patrol attendant to inspect any suspicious movements around the section of the region. He was wondering how he would be received. Arriving at the residence, he got back to his chamber. No body questioned him. Or maybe none noticed his absence. All in all, he felt the delight of following his instinct and getting out of the army borough for a self-rewarding reason.

After building resilience to the malaria, he had a whole week of intensive training. His physique had adopted to the routine of the camp in a strange way. Like they say, when you catch a malaria, that's when you adopt to living in the jungle. An early morning bath, followed by tea with mostly dried bread and occasionally doughnuts, jogging and fitness practice then resting into the chores of the day. He felt a revitalisation to cope with any inducements to capitulation. His virtue and zeal had surfaced.

After recovering from the malaria and gaining his energy, Anwar began to feel peculiar in the camp. The compact kitchen was not a convenient setting for them. They were used to tea-drinking under thatched sheds. Everybody took off him whenever he approaches. He can't explain better that he didn't burn the cookhouse, and Hamid couldn't give any explanation at all. So he went around looking for Maher, who had been more welcoming. He walked *shaw-shaw* as if on a desert sand. He stopped beside Maher on a drenched ground beside the burnt shed.

'Careful, careful!' Maher yelled, pointing on the wet ground beneath. He had already stepped into the mud.

'I can put up a better shed', Anwar said, taking some steps from the wet ground.

'This is exactly what I was waiting to talk to you about, let's go and bring some equipment'.

'Are we going into the market?' Anwar asked.

'No, the thatches are plenty over here', Maher replied.

'Okay, let me change to casual', Anwar said.

'No, no need to. You are not going to carry it on your head. We will find a carriage', Maher replied.

They walked down the hill from under the dense trees into the main road. The alleyway was an ordinary receptacle of a paved pictorial contour into the town's neighbourhoods.

'Thatch grass are plenty in this side of the country', Maher said. 'It is the season when the locals would collect them in their yards as stock for their manufactures', he continued.

Contrary to his previous observations, Anwar realised that Maher was a talkative person. They walked a few kilometres from their residence to a compound stocked with bundles of thatches, piles of logs, and folded mats. Anwar was looking around in amazement at the marvel's pale reflections of the dry supplies.

'Hey', Maher said.

'There are no thatches, these ones are not even enough for the hut I am building'. It was Ufindi, a very slender light-skin-toned young lad. He was very sweaty and seemed to be a hardworking fella.

'How did you know we are here for some thatch', Maher asked.

'We saw the smoke. Did you see the poles pulled off the place where the shed had burnt when you returned from jogging?' Ufindi asked Maher.

'Yeah, we did see that', Maher said. 'You drenched the yard'. The army was known to being so annoyed of going back to normal people seeking help. They would rather forcefully takeover something than ask for help.

'We were the ones who put the rest of the fire off and pulled the wooden poles to the side', Ufindi continued. 'Let's make a deal, we will build it for you, and you pay for the labour'.

'We just need the thatch, and we can build it ourselves', Maher replied. He tapped on the bundle of thatches beside them and looked to Ufindi. 'Don't you think we are the men enough for the job?'

'Ha, when was the last time you have been to the front line?' he asked, looking at Maher. 'I heard you ran from the rebels'.

Maher didn't like the mention of his return from the front line. It was an experience that was harsher than the battleground. He had spent weeks with anxious nights and daily nervous breakdown to overcome this. 'You give us the thatch, or we take them by ourselves', he responded furiously.

'Don't threaten me, Maher, you try, and I will crunch you to the ground', Ufinidi responded. Everybody was quiet at the sudden-heated discussion. 'There are so much in the forest, take a cutter and collect from there'. Ufindi walked back to where he was resting under the shed.

The two soldiers stood in the yard, watching him walk away. At that moment, Utaz Khamis pedalled in with his bicycle. He parked it by the entrance. Seeing the two men, he called out to Ufindi, 'Ufindi, Ufindi'.

'Yeah', Ufindi responded from under the shed.

'You have people here waiting for you'. He strolled to where they were standing whilst he glanced around the place. 'Salam aliekum', he said with a handshake. 'Welcome to the shed, the sun is burning hot today'.

Ufindi was under the shed, cleaning the lantern for the night. 'We have talked', he said, holding a ragged towel, with which he was removing the precipitations from a cylinder glass.

'Welcome', he called the soldiers to the shed. 'Let Sonia make some tea', he continued, turning to Ufindi.

'Maher, I have not seen you in a while. Are you looking for something?'

'They left their shed to burn down, now they are looking for thatch', Ufindi said mockingly and walked out of the shed.

Maher looked at him and responded, 'I was not there'. He knows Ufindi and was very cautious to have a peaceful approach. Else, they won't get what they came for, so he turned, shaking his head, and looked to the ground.

'Who was there? It can't burn by itself', Ufindi continued from the distance.

'Anwar, welcome', Ustaz Khamis responded, trying to break the endless arguments. 'In this place, the unexpected happens anytime, and people just go on living'. They all laughed at the joke.

Ufindi returned walking to where the three men sat under the shed with a silver tray on one hand and a tea thermos on the other.

Their argument was settled that they can collect the thatches for their shed without any cost. The base had defended that side of the town from random attacks. And in times of droughts, the locals would fetch water from the water pump in the compound of the army hostel. For Uncle Khamis, there were more unconventional mutual reimbursements to being in good terms with their nemesis neighbours, the army.

WAU, THE TOWN

That same week Anwar had accompanied a travelling colleague with Tom to the airport, where they dropped a returning officer. On their way back, they passed by the main garrison to meet *naqib* Santino. They did not stay there long, fearing an encounter with the *liwa*. From the main garrison, they took a different path from the main intermission of their usual route towards the town's stadium. They preceded towards a sideway track on the Northern boundary of the town. Passing the fascinating sights of the town, Anwar turned his head to the side to see the town acutely entrenched in the splendour of the great jungle extending adjacent to a peripheral bridge. A curve of hard wooden trees abounds on one side of the street. Whilst to the forefront of their derive was displayed a frontispiece into the town, Wau Downtown. It was a mysterious tranquillity that spurred in Anwar, a profound adoration for the piece of the country he never knew before.

They arrived in a quite location lined by trees clasped in the oldness of their growth. They went and stationed under some of the dense trees by a wholesale merchant's shop that opened to a major avenue; a route conventionally positioned to emerge from the river on the east, a prime location in connotation of the town's foundation. He could feel a slightly different breeze, humid, relentless, but gentle and filled with the impervious scent of a coastline.

He can see as many Northerners as he would in any souk in a Northern town, a total refinement of the North in a Southerly setting. On a walking path beside the main road, countryside women arrived, carrying woven baskets filled with harvests. Countless passers-by ride on bicycles hustling on bumpy meandering paths. The haze of mobilities, the spectra of shops on the open porches, occupied the sight. That part of town fascinated him. What had struck his attention the most was that piece of the country was actually not just a remote location. It was inhabited, constructed, sophisticated, and dynamic. He can feel the vivacious power of able-bodied men and women actively moving around their businesses as they mind their interests. Nonetheless, he did not fail to observe the obvious signs of obscured hostilities on some fierce, worn faces walking the streets.

'Hey, look here', Tom summoned from his driver's seat. 'You will get used to everything you see in town soon'.

They arrived to one of the members of the chamber of commerce in town who wanted to meet Anwar. After the encounter with the chief military commander *liwa* Abdel Azeem, he became a sought-after name. Significant individuals in town would seek and initiate ways to meet him. He learnt about this man Amu Mahdi from Tom. Though they don't get along so well, Tom agreed to go with Anwar to meet the person.

'How did you recover from the malaria?' asked Amu Mahdi, the owner of the shop. Amu Mahdi was a nickname of Abbas Ser Alkhitim as the merchant had become a focal person in the market and one of the references in town, like the treasury of the town's edifice and socioeconomic construction. Obviously, the story of the sickness was accompanying Anwar everywhere he had gone, how he stayed sick for a week and went missing in one of the days. He would just say he went for a walk in the bush. Where they were seated, the narratives of trips to combat zones permeated their conversation. That was an imminent scenario after perching in town.

'That man *liwa* Abdel Azeem', Amu Mahdi began as he sat on one of the chairs under the trees, 'do you know him well?' Amu Mahdi was a stout figured man. He was the owner and the bookkeeper in his shop. On his counter, all financial records are performed. All the labour-intensive works, however, was being done by the loaders. Men carried the goods in and out of the warehouse. The ones that arrived were loaded from a lorry, whilst those that are being distributed are loaded over a horse carriage; a very busy time in the tranquil spectacle of one of the sanctuaries in town.

'No'. Anwar thought carefully about what he would say. 'I only reacted from an expressive impulse of the sight of what was taking place'. He knew he needed not to say more. Amu Mahdi himself was someone; he doesn't know very well yet.

Amu Mahdi took a tiny stick from the ground and started to clean his ears, calling from time to time over for his employees to get the loading of the goods completed. He appeared too reluctant to discuss more about the chief commander's issue. He went on and started talking about the areas around the region. He had been to most part of the region and had founded merchandising posts there. 'You know these goods', he started again, pointing to the lorry, 'they arrived from Raga this morning'.

'Yeah, I heard the convoys have begun to arrive', Tom said.

'Yeah, this is the season we receive the supply of our goods, any goods, and we sell them throughout the year as the demands arise'.

'I see this is how you stayed in the market', Anwar responded after some silence and pondering what to say.

'Yes', Amu Mahdi responded. 'You know, my son', he continued, giving Anwar a cup of tea, 'to stay in the market, you need to know what the locals demand'.

'But I see that the real locals can survive without most of the goods', Anwar responded. 'Actually, they can live without most of the goods'.

Amu Mahdi said, 'When there were no wars', leaning forward to the table in the middle. The talk of no war enlightens everybody in any public debate. 'I started from Anzara', Amu Mahdi began narrating his story. 'My uncle was an official in the scheme. I accompanied him because I was more drawn to making money than school. I finished preparatory grades and thought that's enough. I have always had a huge build, and my classmates would see me as older than them, though I was younger', he said with a smile. 'When Anzara scheme stopped, I told my uncle I am not going back now. I was only 18 years old then. I went to work as a carpenter in Tonj for five years. Then I had to leave Tonj again. I came to this town in the late '80s and never left since then. I have my family here, and my children are grown'.

'This is quite an autobiography', Tom said.

'The more you stay in this town, the more you won't desire to leave', Amu Mahdi said. 'Right, Anwar?' he said laughing.

Anwar smiled and nodded, totally convinced of what he was hearing as he too had begun diving into the depth of staying in the town.

Just then Sarah, with her elder sister, came walking to the shop. As beautiful as he had seen her, what should he say? She gave a letter to Amu Mahdi, whom he found was a good acquaintance of Uncle Khamis. He got up from the chair he was sitting on and greeted them with a handshake, a gesture of respect. She smiled and said, 'We are just picking some things and leaving'.

'Tea then?' he asked.

'No, we are not used to drinking tea in the marketplace', she responded. Briefly, what they came for, a set of dry groceries in a box, was parcelled for them to carry home. As they walked away, she turned and smiled at Anwar who was obviously overtaken by the incidence of their coming. They were all quiet after the beautiful commotion.

Amu Mahadi kept an eye on Anwar as the girls walked away. 'Be careful', he started talking, 'she is not an easy girl. She is a friend to one of my daughters. I have put my children with the nuns' schools to learn English'. He looked at Anwar and continued, 'If you are serious, be serious. She is a girl with an optimistic future. Don't interpose that'.

Anwar was quiet. To make things fair, he went on, 'I also see that you are a gentleman yourself. Though the military career can be considered as a total catastrophe when contrasted to a white-collar job, I strongly encourage you to decide against all odds'.

Then he went on explaining his time around the region again. He was in Tonj, a town to the southeast. 'Tonj was a raw mixture of the villagers and the posted officials', he said. 'I stayed there for a while, travelled to Mapel, and decided to make my way to Wau'. He sighed with a heavy breath from under his *jalabia* with the stick still in his hand. His beard was full to his cheeks, and his ears were full of hair. He continued with his narratives. 'I used to go to Raga and arrange to transport my goods from there. The bandits would be around, escorting you on their separate pathways. You think the road was clear, but no, you just keep your calm. They would make up their minds whether to take your goods or not, until you become a travelling acquaintance from season to season'. They all laughed. 'Imagine being escorted by the burglars of the jungle until you arrive at the edge of the town. One season they helped us hunt a troubling rhinoceros. It was tough to slay and was even chasing us. At the end, we divided the hunted meat equally'.

Tom got up, stretched his arms, and said, 'You know, I will decide to find a wife soon. Returning to the North is not in my mind now. I haven't eaten enough rhinos yet'. They all laughed.

When they prepared to leave, the shops were beginning to get closed. 'Anwar', Amu Mahdi called him as they started walking away. 'Stay out of trouble'. He nodded as they made their way under the trees onto the side where they parked their military wagon.

Their drive back was into the part of the town with phenomenal antiquity. The beginning of their exit was a T-shaped juncture lined in all directions with commercial constructions. Built with absolute ingenuity, the buildings were shaped with careful imprints and uniformed patterns arranged adjacently to each zinc roofs, elevated open porches, walls creased with white paints, and double-sided doors painted either green or blue. Like a child, he was submerged in baptism he was for a little while, overtaken in the humbly sophisticated architectural details.

The winter sun was auspiciously bright and golden, illuminating the empty sky. Dense green trees with very stoutly woody branches proffered over the rustic roofs. They drove beyond the market and past the church with the dome pinnacle, which he had seen on his arrival at the airport. The farther they drove, the more they get to the splendid sights of what the history of the town atoned.

They arrived another juncture, not so broad as the one he had seen during their drive from the airport, then turned right up a hill with a mosque and towards their residence.

It was 7:00 p.m. at their military station. Though just a few kilometres drive from the township, their drive back from the marketplace seemed protracted. As it was winter, the sun downed early as usual. The lantern on the side table was lit as usual. The emitted light beams illuminated the room with the familiar aroma of kerosene.

'First Sergeant Anwar', he heard his name. The voice, though, was the voice of their commanding officer in the residence, Abdel Aziz.

He got out of the room, seeing Brigadier General Abdel Aziz, with hands in his pockets, standing by the African tulip tree adjacent to the building's ingress. He assumed what the discourse would be since he had been with Tom the whole day.

'Yes, sir', he responded with a salute.

'Now I see why they sent you to this confinement', he responded, taking a step towards Anwar. 'Commander Abdel Azeem wrestles. His argument are won with the fists'.

'I—' Anwar tried to respond.

'You what?' He became tempered at him. 'Whatever you learnt, whatever you did, whatever you heard, whatever you said, *all* of them brought you here'. He walked to the other side and continued with a more condensed tone. 'Here, you are meant to reconstruct your inner sense. To redefine yourself and embark on your duty of call. This is the time I get to have a role in your journey. That was why the chief commander didn't respond to your arrogant impulsive reaction. What do you think the army men do in a battlefield?'

Anwar was quiet.

'Answer me', Abdel Aziz said again.

'They fight, sir!' Anwar yelled back. He could feel the sound of his heartbeat pounding very fast.

'Unfortunately'. They were quiet. He then continued, 'The person you were set with to explain these realities is here, so listen to these carefully so you get alive from this confinement. One, you are not to show anywhere, not by chance of arrogant impulses, that you are against your commanders. Two, you are not to create any ties in town. Three, no women. Four, no drinking. Clear?'

'Yes, sir', Anwar responded at the gasp of his breath.

'Now dismissed!' yelled Abdel Aziz. Anwar saluted with attention stand and walked the steps into the room, not looking back.

He pulled off his shirt and singlet at the door and put them over the clothes hanger on the corner. He got to his iron-framed single bed and sat by the side. A cool dry breeze blew through the window onto his back. Feeling the chills on his bare chest, he reached for his shirt on the wooden clothes stand in the corner. Putting his shirt on, he crossed his arms over his chest and remained on the bedside. The radio was randomly narrating as always on worlds so far away from his. Still sitting on the bedside, he started to doze off; he laid his head on the pillow and began snoring right away.

The next day Anwar finished his duty and returned to the room as usual. Taher, a roommate of his, entered the room at the same time. Taher was a slender-figured, bald-headed, medium-height man, probably approaching his fifth decade. They rarely get along. At times they get into exhaustive arguments. And that day was one of the days.

'Oh, the beau is in the house', he said scornfully.

Anwar raised his head, looked at him with pity. 'Tell me', he said thoughtfully, 'are you contented?'

'What do you mean?' Taher asked. 'I work, I receive my salary, yes, I am content'.

'Well, I am not. And that is the difference between your standpoint and mine'.

'Oh, you are talking about social difference, right?' he asked.

'No, I mean difference in how we perceive things. The difference in how each of us strives to protect a higher cause'.

'Excuse me, come on, you have been here for just one month. Now you are already twisted 360 degrees. Man, you are really hooked'.

'Are you aware of why I was transferred here?' Anwar asked with a firm tone. 'I was able to question those in higher ranks than us'.

'I can see your desolation now', Taher said. 'You want to create a world where fairy tales like yours could exist'.

'Well, it's apparent that you and I don't seem to reach any understanding regarding the obvious and pressing matters'.

'I was once your age, so keep your millennial philosophies to yourself', Taher said as he pulled his towel from his bedhead. 'You want an advice from me? Things are different here', he said and headed to the shower room. Whereas Anwar, he had to reflect at himself. Something had to dawn on him if that is how he is being perceived all this period. He thought, shaking his head in disbelief. He got up, went to the kitchen to fetch a cup of tea.

The house steward, Hamid, was in the kitchen, making a stew of dry okra. He could smell the pungent odour of the fried onions as he prepared his tea. Holding his cup, pleasant scents of mint and cane syrup radiated his face. He recalled what the chief officer had said to caution him, *'Here, you are meant to reconstruct your inner sense, to redefine yourself and embark on your duty of call.'* His posting to that base was a deliberate act to tame his growing indignation against those in positions higher than his. But that proved to be hard to accomplish. For he was sent to the forefront and had begun to see firsthand the predicaments at the grassroots. He could comprehend the grounds for their fervent unwavering upheavals. He could identify. His everyday life became an articulation of an uprising against societal injustice. Why wouldn't he? After all, his heart had been caught in the charms of a gazelle.

The other day he had met Sarah in the marketplace at Amu Mahdi's shop. He, a male in uniform; she, a young woman from the local inhabitants. Her dark skin tone and finely plaited hair glimmered under the bright sunlight. She was wearing a flowery tinted dress and some patterned beads. When their gazes met, something in him came to life. Their two worlds reckoned to the call of the heart. They are part of the great society of those who suffered injustice and yearn for peace. He believed destiny had landed him there, so far away from home. He sat on the bedside, with head held on one hand and a cup of tea on the other, contemplating his ordeal.

Every day the morning routine was more rigid. He got all the sequences of the procedures. At that point, his physique had adapted the routines he just smashed the shoves with no restraint. He had to look beyond that time and adjust the mind to a steady predisposition to reach a fundamental end. His core, though, was telling him, there was further push to the fight ahead.

He thought of Sarah. It had been weeks since he last met her. It was past mid-December. The days were approaching Christmastime, a favourable season in the locality. One of his plans was to find out how to visit Uncle Khamis. However, after the sequential call to caution, he was not sure how that was going to happen.

The day came when they were to rebuild their shed after it burnt off. They had a good number of team in place. In the heat of the day, they posted the poles and fixed the straws line by line on the sides and hoop by hoop on the roof. He kept working, watching the endless arguments between Maher and Ufindi. Though they never seemed to get along, they have the same energy reclined to getting the job done. The cookhouse was finally in place, and Anwar could pull himself out of the embarrassment of being the awkward addition to the residence. Evening arrived, and the haze in the residence could be sensed, even in their detachment.

When daytime dwindled and night-time approached, his sentiments began to sense that intrinsic pragmatism, and not-conceited opportunism was key to uplifting his integration. They could hear continual sounds of drums carried along in the winter breeze as they sat by the dried tulip tree by having tea with baked biscuits brought to them to celebrate their achieved work. The home-cooked cookies reminded Anwar of Sarah, and he wondered if she would make something good as well. So he began to think of disappearing again and go to their place.

Right after the dark dawned, he realised the commander was not in yet. He knew he was being monitored but decided to escape. He walked the diverged path in few minutes. It was dark and quiet. He prayed that he could meet his lover. He passed Ufindi's canteen from the distance. Since his first meet in that place, he never caught his mockery as clever. As good affluence would atone, he saw Sarah in the distance, picking a small sack of charcoal in front of the canteen. To that point, she hasn't heard from him. He had either to be brave and say it or be brave and be quiet. Both responses were daring for him. Whilst watching, he noticed Ufindi saying something to Sarah's ears that made him feel jealous. His suspiciousness was prompting him to move out of the hiding, yet he had to be more cautious of his moves in those days until things subsided in his residence.

She took the main path to the house as it would be safer. Walking the trails on the road, she heard some footsteps. At first, she thought the sounds were from the houses beside the street. The road was dusky, and she could only see few steps from her position. But the steps grew louder and nearer. She became hesitant to turn and see who might be following her or take swifter steps and run. Again, overcame by her courage, she held the sack up on her arms and close to her chest and moved to one edge of the street. The walker might have realised her gestures because he kept to the other side of the road, almost walking on the grass and few steps away.

'Peace', he said with a deep tone. Sarah said nothing, though she seemed to recognise the voice.

'I said peace, and you did not respond', he said.

She looked at him and smiled. He could see her bright teeth in the faded glow of the way. He went on, 'When someone says peace to you, then that is good because peace is something good'. She was quite again; he wondered if she might not be that interested in him as he thought.

'Sarah', he called.

'Yeah', she responded.

'I can't be seen talking to you', he said. 'I would be suspended'. She was quiet. 'Can we take another path?' he asked. He took big steps past her marching, *shaw-shaw-shaw*. He was wearing leopard leather shoes, which normally doesn't make a sound, but since he was a desert walker, that was not possible. She followed him to where she could see their house from a close distance.

'You are not coming in?' she asked with annoyed tone.

'You don't talk to me', he said.

'Why did you say we can't be seen talking?' she asked. 'What did I say to you?'

'No, no, it had nothing to do with you', he responded. He put his hand on her shoulder as they strode the lone pathway. 'I had so much trouble lately', he said.

'What sort of trouble, Anwar?' she asked.

'I want to tell you everything from my heart, Sarah', he said.

'Then tell me', she responded strongly.

'You are too young for me, dear', he said and removed his hand off her shoulder.

'What's in your heart that I need to know?' she asked. He was quiet.

'You', he said and stopped walking as they were by the fence.

She turned over to him. 'We are staying late tonight to bake Christmas biscuits'.

They were quiet. He broke the silence and asked, 'Do you make good food?' he asked.

'Try me', she responded

He took a step forward and kissed her forehead, something she wasn't expecting. They were quiet. She took steps back and walked to the house.

THE PLAINS OF BUSSERI

When he returned to the residence, he found a note stuck on the handle of his Panasonic radio, stating that the next day he had to report to another station out of town for a couple of weeks, replacing a sick army official. He wondered, *Could all these be made up?* He almost tore the note. But he didn't tear it, thinking lest they demanded it from him. He pulled his travelling bag, collected his clothes from the handler, and folded them into the bag. He set his luggage ready, except for the pyjamas he was wearing, the radio, and his uniform. He was all set to leave. He decided not to object in acknowledgement to being accountable to what his journey commanded.

The night had an astonishing inaudibility. In the hushes, the drums seemed to beat in far-flung dialogues; when one distant sound stopped, another one arose in response. How astute if such treatise could pattern a call to a better time, at least one where true love existed. *When love veneers it,* he thought, *it prompts the capacity to elude from hate. Hate would become so insolent and aloof. War zones convert into meeting grounds, where those wanted to be in peace could be noticed. The convergence of love is impartial. It can't be defeated in any of battlegrounds.* He realised the radio was off, and it was him talking to his own consciousness. What time could it be? Without knowing the answer, he started to doze off.

He woke up at dawn as usual. It was Christmas Day in town. He got off his bed and went to the bathing area, where containers were lined. All the water was used up; the remaining amounts were masses of sludge, except for one barrel. He had to bend it to the side to collect the water into a bucket. That was the situation in winter seasons: Water shortage was everywhere. After a cold bath, he returned to the room and put on the full suit uniform and walked through the corridor into the front porch and out in the yard. He stood by the tulip tree. Some tiny bulbs were protruding from the nodes. It was bearing green again. The emerging light of daybreak begun to enthuse his desolate heart. He could smell fresh fragrances of the morning time, disseminating aroma from the tulip tree. What would he say to the girl he pronounced his love to? His mind started to wonder.

Tom dashed out and stood beside him. 'I see you ready for the day', he said.

'Are we travelling together?' Anwar asked.

'Apparently', he said as he walked off to the porch. 'Tea?' he yelled at him.

'It won't be ready in time', Anwar replied.

'No, I have a kerosine stove', he said as his tone diminished on the other side.

He pulled out a cylinder hair comb from the upper pocket of his army shirt to comb his hair.

In just few minutes, Tom arrived with a cup of tea. He handed it to him and walked away into the building. He took the cup and had a sip. It was overboiled, and the cup smelt like kerosine, the most disgusting taste in a cup. He walked to the kitchen, put the cup on a bench without saying anything. In another couple of minutes, Tom came out with a full army suit, and they were ready to leave.

The drive from their camp to their next station took them more than an hour, though the distance was less than 2 miles away. They took a path from their residence southwards beyond the town. Wau was not like any town he had been to in the country. Every direction they moved, he could see a clear amalgamation of histories, revolutionary movements, and culture in the transiency of the town's growth. All along their area, with exception of their residence, there were no colonial constructions. They traversed into a very broad red street coming from town at a major juncture, the Jaw Market. He could see grey contours of woven thatched fences standing laterally by the highway. It was like an imprint of diligence seeing that this part of the town had been nurtured by its people and their eagerness to making it a home to inhabit and relish their cultures. He looked to where the road might lead; it was an endless extension to where his sight could only see the red dust over the skyline. As they exited the town, he heard the church bell from the cathedral ringing in the distance.

He had supposed where he stayed had enough thick forest, not until they took off for a mile. All clasped by the roadside were shrubs and shrubberies. They drove onwards until they got to where there were only trees evergreen and countless. The brightness of the day divulged in him an intrinsic fondness to the region. He turned to Tom who was driving quietly. He decided not to initiate a conversation, lest it gets into an argument. They arrived at the first stop, where they met a young man who wanted to get to Busseri. He was sitting under a tree with his luggage in a sack beside him. Tom and Anwar went into the post office to get their exit permit. They returned and found him sitting.

'Where are you going?' Anwar asked. The young man was quiet.

'Leave him. He will become a responsibility', Tom said as he stood nearby. They walked to the car to continue their journey.

'Busseri!' he yelled from the distance.

'Come over!' Anwar yelled back.

'He is going to be your responsibility. You need to know that', Tom warned.

He came close to the car, threw his luggage inside, and climbed on the back. 'Come and sit in the front', Anwar continued with his generosity, neglecting Tom's cautioning. 'What is your name?' he asked.

'Juma', he replied.

They flocked to the empty red road into Busseri, a significant district of Wau municipality. Established around a technical school, it had the most serene countenance with collections of history and ordinary prettiness. Tiny sketches of foot paths persisted in a total sparseness of passages between sturdy brick houses.

The route to their residence conceded through the largest building in the district, Busseri Church, one of the monumental marks of the Catholic mission in the country. It was an admiration to see the dedication of the missionaries as represented in the establishments.

'This is Busseri Church', Juma said, pointing to the building they were approaching. 'People are inside for the Christmas mass. That's why you don't see anybody around'.

'This part of the country has historic sights. They have obviously put so much effort in place', Anwar said. 'Is your family here?' Anwar asked, turning to Juma.

'No', he replied, scratching his hair.

The two men looked at each other.

'Where you picked me, beyond the post station', he said, looking at them.

'This is what I was talking about', Tom said angrily.

'I want to go to Wau, but I feel sick to walk the distance, so I waited for a car', he replied.

'But you are taking the opposite direction', Anwar said.

'I am going to get there when the car returns later', he replied.

Anwar looked at Tom. 'Are you returning today?' he asked astonishingly.

'Yes, this car brings the ration and returns the same day', Jumma responded.

He was set up to be in the training confinement at BusserI, an area 2 miles further. Since his impulsive attitudes would not conform in situations of relative lenience. The camp was meant to guard the town and support combat zones when need arise, that was going to be his new role.

Anwar was mystified at the substitution setup. He felt so aggravated. He began to feel very anxious of what might follow. They parked the car in an open ground in the new residence. He pulled his bag from the car, looked at Juma, and said, 'Every year and you are good', and walked off.

'May God inscribe peace on your journey!' Tom shouted at Anwar as he knew he was annoyed at the arrangement.

'First Sergeant Anwar FadlaAllah Fareed', an officer called from amongst some few men standing in the compound. He saluted and greeted him. 'I am Major Kosho', he responded with a salute, 'the assistant officer'.

'Who is the chief officer?' he asked.

'*Muqaddam* Aleco Angelo, and *naqib* Mario Hassan is the training officer', he answered. 'They are at the Christmas mass. It is Christmas today, and they will have a long prayer'.

The obvious indicators of his new residence were proper construction and actually a former school building. He noticed the replicated total robbery to the essence of the institution. He had to bear the shame, one way or the other, being a Northerner and in the military. This had set him to a new rage, knowing that perpetual silence had its limits at some point.

He was taken to a room that was the size of a hall, lined with metal beds. Beside each bed was a packed army luggage, except one—that was his bed.

Kosho walked him to his place. 'Two things you need to keep in mind', he said as he walked out. 'One, military life is about orders and self-control. And two, it is about finding a way to get things done at the same time'.

'Well, thank you, my friend', he responded with a heaving gasp as he loaded his luggage down beside the bed. He walked out and sat under a tree with few more comrades playing dominoes. The other comrades he met were *naqib* Jimy, *naqib* Albadwie, *naqib* Sebit, *naqib* Majdi, and *naqib* Ayom. With his bewilderment, he just capitulated the predisposition to cultivate his flexibility after the order of his new dispatchment. He greeted all of them and sat beside watching the day unfold into sundown.

Muqaddam Aleco and *naqib* Mario returned from the Christmas celebration. Aleco, the commanding officer had a very calm persona. While *naqib* Mario the trainer, was very talkative. He had rigid body build, medium height, sparse grey hair, and a young outlook. Some women brought dinner from the Christmas celebration, and he was loudly taking to them from the distance.

'I am *naqib* Mario', he said to Anwar.

He got up and they saluted one another. '*Raqib awwal* Anwar', he replied.

'We are not town buddies', *muqaddam* Aleco said as he they shook hands. 'We are here for the front lines'.

Night-time arrived in another first day in a camp. This part of the world, though, had an absolutely distinctive atmosphere. The smell of the wild was a continual alteration of scents of reptiles and flying insects. He could see the light fly roaming the space of the hall. Mysterious sounds from unidentified creatures in the woodlands would abruptly infiltrate the stillness. He dared not think about his acquaintances in Wau. He wasn't sure when this trial would end. The thought of them added to his predicaments. His heart yearned for more encounters with the girl in whose company his desolation had found closure.

Another first day of training in a camp—his bed was set in the same room opposite *naqib* Mario's. He had a retro alarm clock with metal bell that could wake the entire compound. Besides that, he would blow a rustic brass whistle called *zumbara* like nothing happened. He wore the whistle constantly like a rosary. *Kringring! Kringring! Kringring!* followed by *Wiir! Wiir! Wiir!* was enough to set them alert off the bed. Everybody would rush to get ready. There were ample spaces for bathing for a batch of 50, inclusive of every army personnel in the district. All before 7:00 a.m, their routine functions were intensive.

Their chief instructor, *naqib* Mario—he had no idea which part of the Sudan he was from—was lenient but rigid in the field. He was friendly but rigorous in his commands. He would blow the whistle early, at 6:00 a.m., to call them for training each day of the week. At every whistle, all trainees had to wake up, pack their luggage for standby, then take the morning tea. After that, they would get to the training ground.

The first two weeks included strenuous physical activities. They would march to and fro and crawl for an hour in the compound to build physical competence and resilience. On other schedules, they would jog into the depth of the jungle and back. The singer was *naqib* Albadwei, medium height, dark skin tone, and slender-looking figure. He had strong vocals, would raise the morals of the trainees to jog around the district and back.

From the active suburb, it was anticipated to be at its induction; the war had shrunk Busseri to be a very quiet locality. Busseri was too restricted, detached, and solitary. There was only one road from the town, passing sideways and heading southerly. And another one with disappearing trails branched from the main road at the town's exit point reached Busseri and extended parrel to the main road. Beyond the residences is BusserIi River, a calmly flowing stream. It meets the Jur River, creating a fertile valley east of Wau town. Close to the bank of the river at Busseri wasa charcoal-baking place with protruded earth mounds leaking with smokes from the distance. The houses were distant and dispersed. He realised the residents themselves were so reserved. The locality was so quite most of the time that day with the exception of sounds from a place he had recognised as his new residence. There were no leisure places in the area, except for the superb sights of sunrises and sunsets. There was only one marketplace and one cooked food merchant in the market. They call her Aunt Yang-Awa. She had calmness about her and a caring heart. She makes the best tea with doughnuts. They are only allowed to go outside their compound once and during the day. That was the time he would go to Aunt Yang-Awa's place for tea, day after day, to drench his distresses.

Only two radios operated in the compound: One belonged to *Naqib* Mario, and the second belonged to Anwar. The weeks unfolded to a month. Their routines remained stringent. The only way out of the place was to accomplish the mission of his drafting. One day the news informed of defeated attempts on their side in one of the very contemptuous areas that lay far beyond their district. *Muqaddam* Aleco was sent an information of the defeat besides he was ordered by the chief commander in Grinity *Liwa* Abdel Azeem to support the combatants at Bo Bridge.

First thing in the morning parade, *Muqaddam* Aleco stood before his team to inform them of the news. 'Our troops were prompted to evacuate', he started. 'And we are to substitute the losses in the front line at Bo Bridge', he told them. 'We need to be more prepared, no risking failure, no turnoff', he continued. 'We are now waiting for replacement at Busseri . . .' He paused. 'Until we take off, everyone is needed to be very vigilant and on a persistent standby. Thank you', he ended.

They began the second level of their training. They were to build more trenches for hiding. That day they took off to cut wood logs from the forest around. Sent in sets to look for one another, they all walked in successive teams down the plains to where a river runs northeast. It was the New Year. They walked to the shrubs to cut some leafy branches for a moat they were going to build. Again, a very quiet day, and the breeze was cold and whizzy, a reminiscence of the day he met Sahara at the market. Without noticing, he was in tears. He had to rub it off. Kosho noticed him from the distance and walked to where he was struggling to cut the branches. 'Look here', he said to Anwar as he lifted his axe and plugged off a branch. 'Should I know what was wrong?' he asked.

'No', he responded aggressively and walked off to another shrub.

They worked their muscles off that day to build more hiding trenches. The following days, the roof covered them with thatches, then they loaded the branches over for hiding. From that time on, all the schedules were directed by the escalation of circumstances around. Busseri became bleak in his sight. He could not salvage a drive back to town.

In preparedness for front-line battleground, the days were squashed with rigorous trainings and maximum vigilance. Wau had been one of the strategic targets of the rebels and the government simultaneously. It had borne the dreadful cost of war on its people, their livelihoods, and institutions. The social fabric had been alienated from one another again and again. Where they stayed was an evident breakdown of a development program and a hint into the expense of war.

They were set with the functions of scouting the area and guarding that entry location to town around the hours. They would set the training ground like the conditions they were likely to face in the battleground. Field marches with tactical manoeuvres and returning to trenches. Route marching was an important part of the training. There was a code: nyuge piny. Anwar heard that and realised it was the language Ayom spoke.

At their resting time, he went to Ayom. 'I am going for tea at Aunt Yang-Awa's', he said.

'Let's go', Ayom responded.

They arrived at the only market in place, sat in chairs outside the shed in the delight of the evening. Some women passed by, coming from the route that led into the forest. They were carrying loads of firewood on their heads. 'These-these', Ayom started, 'these are fighters, don't think of marrying any of them. They shoot like men, I tell you, you can't contend them'.

'How do you expect them to be like in a place like this?' Anwar asked.

'Women like these are married off to commanders. At least they needed them for their ruling', Ayom said jokingly.

'Where is your family, Ayom?' Anwar asked.

'My family?' he asked and paused. One of the customers brought in some raw tobacco they call *gumsha*. They all had the *gumsha* and started talking of stories of war.

'My family are in Kakuma camp in Kenya', Ayom said. 'I have another wife in Wau. My house is in Hila Jadid on the way to Grinty'.

'You see, war is not good', the man started. He was from the locality. Ufiew was his name. 'We just end up fighting ourselves. This place was a boarding school in the '70s. It was a good training scheme. Now see, it's occupied by the army', he said angrily. 'I saw many army men travel these roads. I have been here long enough to recall not all of them returned'. He paused then continued, 'You see these chants you sing every day, they alter your moral, and you go there wholly, at some point ask yourselves what should come next. It has been many years already'.

'Yaba', Ayom started, 'your time is different from this time. The mistrust of the leaders, tribalism, and greed showed up quickly. Even out there, they are fighting amongst themselves as our people here are doing'.

'You see, Anwar', Ayom continued, 'if you came a few years ago, you won't see me or somebody of my sort at this side of the town. If that happened, that would be unusual. A battle can break out'.

'That must be a severely agonising reality', Anwar responded.

'It was terrible', Ufiew responded. 'I won't even survive in his side of the country'.

It begun to get dark, and they had to return to the compound. Going back to their place, Anwar hesitated to ask Ayom what the phrase 'nyuge piny' meant. But then he asked just in case it was something he needed to learn.

'In the jungle, when you hear this phrase, just sit down', Ayom explained. Their minds were whirling with the *gumsha*. Was it the illusion of the *gumsha* or prudency or both combined? Whichever would apply, it was a staggering apprehension to what occurs in the battleground.

'You good?' It was Ayom.

'I am okay', Anwar responded.

'I did not sleep properly last night', Ayom said.

'Where have you been in the evening?' Kosho asked.

'We were with Yaba Ufiew', Ayom said.

'Don't tell me he gave you some of his *gumsha*?' Kosha said.

'He did', Anwar responded. 'I could feel my head spinning 'til the morning'.

Contrary to most indications to fear living with the Southerners, the South was not just a jungle of illiterate men and people walking unclothed. Those were people he would relate to in their individual scuffles. He related to how they endured the prejudice and the insensitivities that perpetuated the war. He shared the frustration and the rage.

The news on the radio was not optimistic of the situations. In the early morning, they would spend time with *naqib* Mario, planning how they were going to reach the combat zone. That time of the year was the season to traverse on the indefinite roads of the jungle. In few more weeks, the roads would be flooded, adding more wrench to the efforts of the combat zone. The jungle life became second to nature, walking to the plains of Busseri River became part of their marshal routines.

It was February. It was an afternoon march. An easterly waft passed from the other side of the river very vagrant and cold. Anwar took a respite by the forward-flowing tributary. No longer fearful, he had attuned; no longer oblivious to the reality of the struggles of war. The reality was him reaching a patent discernment of the discrepancies that war had framed. It was restraining his perception as sharp as the parasite sting of malaria he had felt. It leaves the body wrecked and the mind superficial. It lends willpower to vengeance and bareness to the soul, so much that people could only feel the fever.

Unfortunately, he was not invincible to the replicating melancholy. All that he could do was pronounce the inclination to anticipate and perform otherwise. They marched back with more chants, lifting their Kalashnikovs in the air. 'All hopes rest on Bo Bridge', they chanted with screams louder and louder. Their scattered vocals travelled with the blowing winds across the plains of Busseri.

THE BATTLE OF
BO BRIDGE

The ride was on the top of a military wagon in a line of a military convoy along the red road from Busseri, a distance that seemed incessant for Anwar from the cringe of his military journey. That was a continual unwrap of the red soil beneath the grasslands. The shrubs were denser, and the weather overcast humidity with sweatiness from the blistering sunrays. They arrived the first station after a long drive out of Busseri. It was a location off a village called Beringi, around 20 miles south of Wau. They met another consignment of Beringi sector. It was a maniac venture. They were delayed for a week at Beringi. They encountered a problem at their arrival. Two militants went missing with their armaments. They subverted the surrounding woodlands in search of their traces. They were not found. They had to wait for a week to supress any defects.

Like any war situation, the locals endured the impact of the defection. Every night was a speculation of what might happen if they showed back to the district again. Though a very small locality and some distance off the main road compared to Busseri, they had to station in it to normalise the route back to Wau. Night patrols started in the evenings before sunset, and any movement was a suspected mutiny.

They spent night after night sleeping under the twinkling sky beside their convoy at the mercy of the unknown wild. He had observed that in the region's arrangements, war was not in supposition as the native residents had adopted merchandising in their agrarian livelihood. In their touring, they found sets of militias in their respective ethnic localities who served as citadels of their respective areas.

He had one phrase in mind, a phrase that, to him, redefined the countenance of the protracted struggle of the Sudanese. In the act of strenuously unwrapping how people related and the process of getting into the depth of the story, the different communities either alienated one another or forcefully crossed one another's boundaries, and thus, war became the ultimate exchange. That was an unmistaken revealing to that vicious occurrence of conflicts. Furthermore, there was no objective line of who the enemy was in person.

Anwar noticed how the drive to war was such a contagious experience pushing the communities to disputes. He met sons of the South going to fight against their own compatriots. That demanded a question to be raised: Who was fighting who? It was an equivalently important discernment for him. Though he can't speculate for everyone, it was inevitable in the process to emphasise the existence of a very diverse society within the bigger diversity. When would it end was another monumental contemplation. Or rather, when would each perceive the existence of the other as ordinary to that scope of time?

The day they were to leave had arrived; dinner was prepared at their camping site. After their farewell meal, he went and sat at the only canteen beside their stationing break. The trader called Adam was obviously from the West from his distinctive accent. He sells a pleasant-smelling tea.

'How much is a cup?' Anwar asked Adam.

'You like tanaka?' he asked Anwar.

'I had drunk much tea at this side of the country than anywhere else', Anwar replied.

'Where do you come from?' Adam asked.

'Khartoum', Anwar replied.

'The front line is harsh. Be prepared for the worst: the weather, the wild animals, and the rebels. The car can get stuck on the road for days as the weather changes. Now is a good season to travel. Make sure you have sufficient ammunitions'.

'I have been stationed in many locations but haven't got to any confronting zones', Anwar told him.

'Depend on God. You survive this, you will survive anything', Adam told him.

'How much do I owe you?' Anwar asked.

'Pay me when you return', he responded. They tapped each other's shoulder, and Anwar went to report himself to his team as they prepare to depart. Now that he found himself on the second part of his perception of the reality, how would the front line look? As Adam had informed him, he should imagine a forest wilderness. In that, every human should survive at all costs.

Finally, they took off Beringi late in the evening, driving slowly and vigilantly in the dark. The night was still. The hush replicated the ghosting sounds of the wild. The land was as wide and vacant as the sky above. He was in an inexplicable mental dispute. The clutch to life was a fight of its own. First station after Beringi is Zingwanda. It was without any suspicious encounters. So they decided to proceed that night to Peili to secure their locations for battle.

Just a mile away before Peili, they got into a heavy ambush. It was something most of them hadn't experienced before in their military career. Bullets flew at every direction. They had to withdraw from the main path to the jungle and hide behind rocks and shrubs for the night 'til morning approached. It was a wait beneath heavy fumes and dust. Some bullets flew very close to their feet. None of them knew where the rebels were hiding in the bush. After all, the rebels were better acquainted to these woodlands. It was the lengthiest wait to move from one spot to other. Slowly, the sounds of the missiles reverted to the distance.

They spent the night digging trenches six feet wide and a moat six feet deep and as big as a room to retrieve to in any ambush. They lost comrades, and some were heavily injured. Very early morning the next day, one of their aid vehicles had to return to Beringi with the injured. The rest of them had to carry on, or the entire region would be set at risk of being occupied by the opposing combatants.

Following that were days spent in hiding or marching and crawling in the bush to reach Peili. The rebels had already taken the advantage of the ambush. As for them, they had to retrieve or go for combat. They decided to fight. The day of their combat, the intensity of war was too unbearable. Bullets were skyrocketing like wasps on every direction. There was no control over any action. It was an articulation of the rule of fear and of retribution, two whole days of continuous confrontation, they moved on leaving all the unknown names collapsing for a required conquest. Lives were lost at one move or even a hiss. Stiffing and coughing of those at the brink of life and death ascended from the ashes of men's insanity. There was a silence at the aftermath of that fierce battle, the silence of devastation and ruin, where the beauty of the wild was laid bare under smouldered remnants of living beings. Anwar sat on a ground by a running stream, looking blurry as he regained consciousness.

'This is the war zone. Now get up and find your luggage', someone spoke from beside him. It was Kosho. 'You got to tell that fear it is not over yet', he continued.

They had reached Bo Bridge. A distance that could otherwise be covered in a day from Wau town had costed days and lives. In the midst of the chants, he had the sensation of getting to a pursuit and discovering that the situation demanded further effort. All that which was achieved was not enough. At that point, he began questioning wherefore he was into this. As a mere soldier, he was subdued by orders. Where could his solace be? He had to reach for the arms of his lover. In the resound of the takeover, his greatest pursuit became love. He walked up to the car, sat on the open back, pulled his cap to his face. He overlooked the scenery at the return trip. It had borne the bloods and lives of unknown souls. Let the journey lead where it would go.

They were cheered at the street as their military caravan passed by Peili and Zingwanda. They arrived Beringi at dusk. He walked straight to Adam at the canteen.

'Hej, Anwar!' he yelled. 'You survived'.

'Thanks be to God', Anwar replied.

'Welcome back', Adam said, shaking Anwar's hand.

'How much do I owe you now?' he asked the shopkeeper.

'Nothing', Adam replied.

'May God reward you with goodness', Anwar responded.

He got back on the wagon, and they returned to Busseri. He chanted back to life to the reprisal power of virtue over the unsound influence of the inclination to war. He had seen what war does. Now in his capacity was the inherent force to fight every battle that would lend conquest to amity.

They finally arrived at the residence at Busseri. They got the chance to find out who from their unit survived. His comrades *naqib* Jimy, *naqib* Albadwie, *naqib* Sebit, *naqib* Majdi, and *naqib* Ayom returned. Their commanding officers *Muqaddam* Aleco and Major Kosho returned.

Naqib Mario walked to Anwar and shook his hands. 'Are you good?'

'I am good', Anwar responded.

'I don't know how far you are going to get from here', he said. 'Even so, God bless you'.

Anwar pulled the iron cape off his head, shook his head to lighten his head, looked at the cape as if he had nothing to say, but then started talking when *Naqib* Mario turned to the rest of the soldiers.

'Why are you saying this?' he asked.

'You know that I am a Southerner with all military skills needed on the other side, yet I remained here training for combat'.

'Why did you remain here?' he asked.

'All efforts ended on the battleground, no which side I stand. Now why I talked to you like that was because we need people who would take the country from the battle front lines to better front lines', he said, looking at Anwar from beyond hazel eyes. They were enervated from insistent futile tactics to the ultimate gain for all causes.

The end of one journey had set the beginning of another journey. The next day the drive to town was a cheery breezy ride past lime-coloured grasslands on both sides of the streets. They bid farewell to the bare assemblies of those projects forsaken to corrode in the magnitude of the dreadful conflicts. It was the inception of the rainy days. They were escorted to Wau by more troops who arrived earlier. The intention was to raise their moral and deceive the citizens in town of the realities in the front lines. He reached Wau. Yet still, his heart was pounding with apprehension. What more might he comprehend? Nevertheless, the dread of the front line was the strongest provoking to finding a pathway to a counteraction.

All along the way, they were being chanted by the residents lining the streets of their convoy. Those were mere people constrained by the need to feeling secure in the complexity of the conflict. He realised that what touches peoples' sentiments was universal. People tremendously related to the force of good over evil, to the triumphs over ruins, to what calls to hope, and devastatingly, to what unites humankind. He too would be carried around by those very same gushes to respond to triumph, hope, and a dignified humanity. He won't question who was behind the call.

They arrived at the military hospital to an extremely different atmosphere, to the screams and cries of those whose loved ones hadn't returned, of those whose loved ones had been handicapped in the clashes, cries to the reoccurrence of desolation and silence over the facts of combat zones. Again, he related. He had experienced the horror. That was why the call for a counteraction was a pursuit worth a try.

He arrived at the residence late that evening in an indistinct dusk. He was warmly greeted and welcomed by his comrades. The place was quite occupied with new admissions being trained to be posted across the region. As a complex by itself, it was not a sufficient accommodation for the rising demand of army recruitments. After his return, his perceptions have been sharply reconstructed, that had added an understanding of the military occupations of residents all through the region.

More than his first night in the camp, he couldn't slumber. He turned from side to side on the bed. The radio was on all night. He can't recall what was being narrated. He was so strained to the demand of that which he can't articulate, rather conciliate, in tender concerns.

THE TULIP TREE

T he next day he woke early and got to the parade. He was called again by *aqid* Abdel Aziz in the morning parade. He marched with every reason to believe that he convincingly fitted into the squad. His trepidation and spontaneity had masked his sight before. He saluted with every conceit, this time with more confidence in his military skills, for indeed, he belonged.

Walking back from the parade, Anwar noticed how the tulip tree was in full blossoming splendour all over the peripheries of its inflorescence. It was in a seasonal rebirth a total contrast to its autumn shape yet equally splendid in presence. After they were dismissed from the parade, they went to have breakfast under its cold shed. They sat in a circle, each of them with equal significance in the military journey. The shed was cold. They talked of the accounts of the front line with a roller coaster of reactions.

At midday, they drove with Taher to the main garrison in Grinty. He begun to view the living conditions with an awareness of the need to influence a change. Grinty, to him, only consisted of few giant constructions and some other structures that housed the military personnel. Most of the lower-ranked officials lived independently around the fringes of the town. As they entered, all over the local stations, the broadcasting was a perpetual incitement of a disposition to conflict. That was the situation of the system in place; they were overprepared for combat, so much that civil culture was discredited.

Liwa Abdel Azeem Andal arrived at the compound at the same time they did. 'Ya *raqib awwal*, Anwar', he called out from the window of his car. 'Meet me at my office'.

'Yes, sir', Anwar replied.

'Contrary to my observation, you were actually skilled for combat'.

'I am, sir', Anwar replied. He was plainly beholding the setting with an audacious judgement; he had overcome one perilous phase as a militant.

'Why did you join the military, Anwar?' he asked. Anwar looked at him, wondering what the appropriate answer would be, lest he placed his call of duty in jeopardy.

'The country is in need of men, sir', he started, 'men who know the country as it is. To procure a sound understanding of everyone's point of view of the war, I had to step out of my civil status to be a military'.

'Now what is your understanding, Anwar?' he asked.

'You know better than me, sir. I do admit that it has taken me a while to transform my mindset to the life of orders and commands. The question is, what do we see many years from now?' he responded.

'I just don't know what is in your mind. Whatever you do, just stay away from my way', he said.

'I am under your command as any of your junior officials, sir', Anwar responded, drawing away from the course of the conversation, lest the *liwa* Abdel Azeem thinks he was after his position.

Where military ranks were influenced by political orders, somebody like Anwar can be placed in a major rank with the slightest experiences.

'I need you here at the head office', he said to Anwar. 'Go and report to *naqib* Santino and get yourself over here. If you remain in Nazareth, you will only be patrolling the town. I would like to assign you to more duties'.

'As you command, sir', Anwar responded. *Liwa* Abdel Azeem nodded as Anwar saluted him. Then they exited the office.

Anwar walked to the storehouse where *naqib* Santino was. 'Anwar, I knew you would make it back', Santino said, rising from his seat.

'I am not only back, but I am also transferred over here', he said as they hugged tightly.

'I now have a resound assurance of having a significant backup because getting here every day is a decision between life and death. Things have escalated so fast, and we are diverged more than ever'.

Anwar didn't know what that meant, but that must have meant something since it was coming from *naqib* Santino.

On their way back to the residence in Nazareth, they passed by the main market in Wau Downtown. Taher was an articulate commuter when it comes to the market. He knows the entire Merchandizing owners. He would roam around from one shop to the next. Anwar went to meet Amu Mahdi at his store. A weave of restored aptitude brightened his face in the shining sun of the early summertime as he approached the shop.

'You reached Bo Bridge and survived?' Amu Mahadi said while greeting him.

'Amu Mahdi, Bo is not any bridge. It is built over a tributary in the midst of nowhere. Even so, it feeds and connects. That could be why we'd have been there'.

'Anwar', somebody called him. He recognised the voice. It was Juma.

'Juma, what are you doing here?' Anwar asked.

'I rented this place', he said, pointing to his shop.

'That is good for you'.

'Do you know Juma, Anwar?' Amu Mahdi asked.

'We lifted him when we were going to Busseri, and he returned with Tom', Anwar responded.

'You did, eh?' Amu Mahdi said in disappointment. 'I brought him to town the same way long time ago. We had disagreement over his wages and moved to another location. Now he returned, and I rewarded him by renting the mill. Isn't that something good?' he asked, looking at Anwar. 'Now I don't owe him anything', he continued.

'Don't say you owe me nothing, how could you say that?' Juma said.

'Look at you, you have a rented mill. Soon you will own it. Isn't that all from me?' he asked.

'You see, Anwar, I earned that', Juma said. He turned to Amu Mahdi and said, 'I carried the grain sacks outside in the mornings and back inside in the evenings every single day even before you had these many loaders. I cleaned the shop, filled the water pot from the pump, and prepared the meal every day. How can you say I don't have wages?'

'Boy, if I didn't offer you a place here, would you have been in this town?' Amu Mahdi said.

'You told me you will cut the rent from the wages', Juma said.

'I didn't promise you anything, but thank God you had a roof on your head all those years', he said.

'But you still owe me', Juma said.

'Now tell me, did Tom put you up for this? If it wasn't for me, he wouldn't have settled in this town in military post every day complaining', Amu Mahdi said.

'No, he doesn't know much of what is going on between you and me. You keep on thinking everything belongs to you. Tell me, what you are doing yourself? You left all the duties for us. We expanded the shop, and today you want to deny all this?' Juma said.

Anwar found himself between a never-ending argument. He tried to divert the talk. 'How was your trip back with Taher that day?' he asked Juma.

'We flew back. Bo is not far from here, you know. any defectors could be in the jungle without being noticed'.

'I could join the rebels if I wanted to, but they don't pay wages. Even in the military, no one pays wages like the Northern divisions'. Juma paused and said, 'Well, I know very well that this shop earns a lot every day'.

'Boy, when did you even learn how to talk?' Amu Mahdi asked.

'People like him say things that not everybody notices', Anwar replied.

Driving back, he was impelled by an obliging need to seek for solace for himself. His sharp instinct had reserved him from the tremors of the front line so far. He also refined his natural appraisal to detaching his emotions after retuning. He had learnt that the hard way. Khamis had been a reflection of an opposite viewpoint in reading the situations in the country, a Southern civilian. He began to feel very whole. For once, he was drawn to the perception that he was genuinely connected to those he was supposed to designate as adversaries. That sense of wholeness was frightening though. He decided not to show what was circulating in his mind. The street was lined by densely tufted growing perennial grasses. The wind was procrastinating an imminent shower. The heat was sweltering. As usual, the drive was that picturesque and quiet.

They arrived at the residence in the afternoon. It was the resting period, and everyone was scattered around the compound. Anwar went to *aqid* Abdel Aziz and found him resting in his room. He stood to salute.

'No, just have a seat', he said, pointing to a chair in the room. 'I have received the report', he said, looking at Anwar. 'I have been conscripted to the Southern divisions and sent to this post and been here meeting soldiers from all parts of the country. What the citizens don't know is that we also ask when the war would cease'. He looked at Anwar again and continued talking. 'The truth, we are to effect that, when you go to those frontiers and never forget the costs that we paid'.

'Thank you, sir'. They stood and saluted each other.

He went out and stood by the tulip tree. The tree was beautiful in all its forms in every season, yet that evening the golden sun added to the flowering tulip a turmoil to the colours of the season, undeniably present and was picturesque. He stood and breathed deeply in the stillness of the sunset. He recalled clearly when he first arrived at that base; it used to look like a wilderness. In the vicinity only dense hardwood trees existed, now emerging with thrilling views of returning meadows. The humidity was very high. He had adapted. The unfolding of the year had proved the residence to be a place as precious as home.

Maher passed by, heading to the direction of the cookhouse. 'Tea, please'.

'Oh, the warrior is back', he chanted, walking to him. 'I told you before, a woman will make a better tea'.

'Are you free?' Anwar asked him.

'Anytime', Maher responded.

They walked to their concealed route to Khamis's place. It was already shrouded with perennial pastures. A thatched fence collapsed on the path from a stormy day. They walked amongst the smouldering vapours from rotten thatches and passed empty yards. Before arriving, Maher thought of asking Anwar about his intentions. 'Hey, Anwar, Sarah is a beautiful girl', he started.

'What are you trying to say?' Anwar asked.

'Be careful if there is anything between you two', Maher said.

'I don't know', he said with a deep breath.

'I am just saying be careful'.

They arrived at the gate.

Sarah came to open the gate; she was staggered by the sudden disappearance and arrival of her guests. 'Anwar, how are you?' she asked. 'Come in', she said, leading the way to the veranda.

They went to their remarkable veranda reception. It was a bright late evening in a season where the days were extended and the breeze carried sweeping voices from the neighbourhood. Sarah was grown in his sight in just the few months he had been away.

'When did you travel without letting anyone know, and when did you return?' Sarah continued talking.

'Sarah', Maher called. "I had also been to the front line since you never asked me any question'.

'No, you disappeared in your hood, Maher', she said. 'We were wondering how you would make it to Bo Bridge'. She turned to Anwar. 'My uncle asked about you, and he learnt that you were already deployed, and your convoy was ambushed'.

'Can I have a cup of tea?' he asked. 'She seemed to know all my moves', he said, turning to Maher.

'I will make the tea', Sarah said.

'However you make it, we will drink', Maher responded, looking for approval at Anwar, who just nodded.

'Where is Uncle Khamis?' Anwar asked.

'He is not in town', Maher responded.

'Where is he?' Anwar asked.

'They all went to fetch charcoal last week before the rainy season gets intensive', Sarah responded.

'Sarah, don't get mad at me for going to the front line. I have been dispatched under orders', Anwar said.

'You know this war had left us miserable, drained, and frightened', Sarah said.

'Do you know that I am on your side?' he asked her. She was quiet. She sat there looking at Anwar. He sensed her resound retribution; she was like a zeal undeniably and was exquisite in the core. To cool her from any rage, he went on talking. 'I see, in a girl like you, beauty and vigour. I see myself. I just hope I appeal to you in any way'.

At that point, Khamis's wife arrived. 'Anwar, my son, I learnt that they sent you to the front line. How are you?' she greeted them. 'Was it not too early for you to go to the front line?'

'That is military life, ma'am. We only respond to orders', Anwar said.

'Maher went three years ago when he first arrived too', she said.

'I will never go to any battleground again', he responded with agitation. 'Nonsense!' he shouted. They know his temperament, so everyone was quiet.

They had dinner at Uncle Khamis's place again, this time with the entire family. The food was so palatable to their taste. The impression was so tantalisingly contented.

In the morning of the next day, he walked out of the corridor to the vibrantly standing tulip tree; its beauty provoked in him a dire composure. He was going to miss watching the seasonal transformation of the tulip. Just as the previous season, it was as naked as a sculpture. He stood under the shed, in the overwhelm of the unfolded realisation of who he was becoming. He thought of Sarah convincingly defying all pertaining odds. Standing there, he enthused that Sarah was his loving soul mate. He couldn't seem to figure out where to start.

'What's the thing about this tree?' It was Taher with his philosophical discussion.

'It stands alone in splendid beauty all seasons', Anwar responded.

Grinity, the main garrison, became his new home. He had begun to appreciate his service as a military personnel. He was upgraded and specified a lodging in the complex. His routine became concrete as he stood the line with high-ranking officials in the region, a new assortment of officials to team with and to mingle with. What happens in their garrison impacts the town and the entire region. His first two acquaintances to his apprehensiveness were two high-ranking officials: *Liwa* Abdel Azeem and *naqib* Santino. That had set him off from the start as an influential member of the squad. He remained in regular interactions with his first team from the other end of the town. The days turned to weeks then into months and to a year and two years.

He decided to settle in the town and begin a private life. His desire was growing intensive as he found that the town had embraced him. That day he went to Amu Mahdi and tried to open his heart to him. He arrived at the main marketplace, where they meet for tea. Amu Mahdi was sitting under the tree with the newspaper unfolded wide. He was reading like a countryside dweller seeing a newspaper after ages. He rolled his face from end to end all over the extended newspaper.

'Amu Mahdi', Anwar called. No response. 'Amu Mahdi', he called again.

'Oh, Anwar'. He folded the paper away. 'When did you arrive, my son?' he asked.

'Just now', he responded.

'Have a seat', he said, pointing to the chairs by his side.

'What is the paper saying today?' he asked.

'Oh, you can't predict', he said, shaking his head. 'We don't know what is going to happen. This is a war region, but the sight of too much arms in town is not a good sign', he said. 'Hey, Juma', he called to Juma who was inside the mill. 'Send for some tea'.

'Okay!' he shouted from inside the mill.

'How did you both get along again?' he asked.

'Haa, you, as long as there is cash flow, we are in good terms. The market is booming now, but the stakes are high', Amu Mahdi said. He looked to the ground and up again. 'What do you think, Anwar, as a military yourself?' he asked.

'When we leave the only option to be armed uprise, this is what we get unfortunately. Every sector of our society becomes armed to be heard. We have enough factions in town to create friction', he said.

'How are you doing there? I know you are straightforward in your talks, but that man, *Liwa* Abdel Azeem, talks good in your face when he wanted to know you well. When he does, he retaliates even with a wrestle'.

'That was what happened when I first met him', Anwar responded.

'He sent some of his men to inform me about that. He had reduced that behaviour now and became more civil in his manoeuvres. He had modified his tactics so much. He used to fight over everything. Haa, this is military, my son. How are you doing in Grinty?'

'Good', he responded. 'Actually, I would like to share something with you'. Anwar began feeling hesitant.

'Go ahead', he said, pulling a table to the middle. The tea was brought in a bright shining metal tray. Its appetizing smell was so soothing, a souvenir of the time he came to this town a couple of years back. It had strong, sweetened cinnamate nuances and a resounding mint aroma. There was something about the marketplace, the shed, and a conversation from the heart. It was October; the last rains have washed the trees, revealing the evergreen vegetation of the savannah. Stationed at the edge of the town, the market was a reception to a raw arrival of villagers. The sun was radiantly shining over the exploding rural returnees. The shades of Africa hadn't been that colourful. Women and girls in dark shiny skin tones, hair braided in fine lines tied to the chin with beads, walked around in shimmering outfits, carrying their produce. Men with heavy-loaded logs and some with sacs walked with running sweats. The arriving villagers were never short of energy. He picked his cup and took a sip in amazement of the liveliness, potency, and zest portrayed in every direction he turned. Then he continued talking.

'You know the family of Khamis who lives on the way to Nazareth', He said to Amu Mahdi.

'Yeah, I know him very well. When they arrived in town, he was staying in the official quarters. When Gonia was being demarcated, he got himself a place then moved there. Now it is boosted with good constructions, especially when the university was transferred to the town. I saw you when the girl came to the market the other day', Amu Mahdi said.

Anwar smiled, decided to speak out.

'She is the one I meant', Anwar responded, looking very pitiful.

'Look, my son, I am not discouraging you. To the Southerners, marriage is a fundamental tradition and is not decided by one person. We are yet to evolve as a society that embrace each other. So everybody's opinion will count. I advise you to talk to Khamis's wife. The women are more helpful, you know'.

'I hear some good news'. Juma walked to them.

'Yeah, Juma, how do you marry a Southern girl?' Anwar asked.

'So much competition, my friend, you can pay the dowry and your rights would be stolen from you. Some people are there to inspect where the marriage is and think that's for them', Juma said.

'Juma, you are discouraging the man', Amu Mahdi said.

'No, I want him to open his eyes cautiously. When they see, you start talking to the girl, they start preparing to steal her the same time you begin. And you also need many men beside you. The flour for the dinner will be on me', he said laughing.

He left the market and went for a visit to the resident in Nazareth before returning to Grinity. Entering the compound at sunset, the tulip tree had never been that blossoming. The red, the green, and the golden trunk were strappingly in a colour tournament of which he was the judge. Though the flowers and the leaves were too animated, the trunk was, in essence, undeniably significant. There was something about Anwar, about his nature, a distinctive gallantness in love, nature, and patriotism. He is the kind that would add spectrum to a place. If the tree could talk, it would speak of a hero in town.

A BATTLE IN TOWN

T he following year was 1997. Anwar had built a strong bond with Khamis and his family. He had begun an undisclosed affection with Sarah, who had reached her high school years then. The year followed the conceptualisation of a concord on peace from within across the country. The implementations of the accords meant the amalgamation of most, if not all, internal forces of the struggles. A major fraction of the armed movement returnees was deployed to Wau for the purpose. He became close to *naqib* Santino, whose role became more challenging and demanded more prudence. That became conflicting with *liwa* Abdel Azeem who was continually deceived by his sources into supposing that his position was at risk. Either an internal rival or the rebel returnee would be more suitable than himself.

In a state of rage, he summoned Anwar to his office. 'The local militia are gaining strong status and getting unified', he started. 'I wonder, where do they get their ammunitions?'

'I shouldn't be the one to answer the question, sir', he responded. After spending years in that side of the country and in the head garrison, he had gained enough confidence to respond with vigour.

'What do you suspect?' Abdel Azeem asked.

'I can't speculate, sir', he answered.

'I ask you to watch out, you are close to *naqib* Santino. When it comes to war, everybody, at some point, takes side. We have to be conscious about that', said *liwa* Abdel Azeem.

'Sir, here, you represent the head of state. If given the choice, would you advice your juniors to take sides?' Anwar asked.

'Military is about orders, Anwar, stop your romantic interactions. Don't think that is not known. We don't decide based on emotional drives'.

'I am not bringing my personal life into this. What are we supposed to report to the government in the North? Should we show the South that the government is against their demand for equality or otherwise?' he asked. *Liwa* Abdel Azeem was stunned at the bold stance. 'Should we consider every demand for fairness as rebellious or external? Some things, orders, don't connote, sir. We have to bring our integrity into what we do, sir'. They were quiet. 'Do you demand anything from me, sir?'

'No', *liwa* Abdel Azeem responded. Anwar saluted and walked to the exit. 'Anwar', he called. 'Just be aware of what is going around, the town is in high tension, and at any point, it might erupt'.

'Sir, if I may speak into this, the offenders are instigated by indiscreet elements from both sides. That is where we have to investigate, if authorised', Anwar responded.

'Keep me informed, Anwar', he responded.

'Yes, sir', Anwar responded with a salute.

Following their discussion, *liwa* Abdel Azeem realised that Anwar had become a threat to his position. The arrival of the Southern militias after the peace talks meant that he could become popular and be given a higher rank for political gains. In a blink of an eye, things might not work for him. He set out his men to follow Anwar's move in town. Without his knowledge, he was being submerged in a plot to remove him from town.

That day he decided to go to Khamis's house after his duties finished. His instinct was telling him something was not okay. So he asked to be dropped a distance way and walked the rest of the route. He dropped off by the mosque on the hill at the interval of the course from the airport. The monumental build had an encompassing view of the town clustered around it in plains, with lanes disappearing beneath magnificent greeneries and rustic zinc roofs. He walked a steep path beside a featured inlay of vast red ground of the freedom square.

It was November again. The breeze was cold on the skin. The sun was gleaming very warm. He wore a casual outfit with a locally made leather shoes and walked, *shaw-shaw*, in the lap of the persistent landscape. The road was seemingly deserted, except for some passers-by and bike riders. He walked in composure, feeling his anxiety vanishing in the travelling winds. He entered the house as he was used to visiting them as one of their relatives. The open porch was overarched with yellowish and dry leafed plants sneaking between the fissures and permeable spaces along the anterior of the veranda as it should at that season of the year. The family had embraced him in his sole journey amongst the unbelievably abrasive armed society.

He found Sarah had arrived home from school. He greeted her with a handshake that had a clutch of attested passions. Their feelings were so introspective, and he felt heartened more than the malaria temperature. He was welcomed into the living room. Sarah walked in, carrying drinking water, and sat on a chair beside him. She had the same passion, though challenged by the truth of who they were as individuals. He picked the cup and quenched his thirst with the whole drink. She sat watching him with an inventive desire to know who he would be without his military status. As if reading her mind, he leaned to her side, held out his hand, caressed her face, and said, 'I am a military man in the South, Sarah'.

Her eyes were telling him a story that motioned his will to overcome. It was a window to that which would enliven his silent screams.

'And I am a Southern schoolgirl, Anwar. I will finish all my school and not leave any part', she responded with daring tone.

'Where is my tea?' he decided to disrupt the lure to her revolting tone.

'Okay, it will take some time because I have to make the fireplace', she said and walked towards the patio to the kitchen.

Anwar sat there, mesmerised of where he could begin with the story. Khamis's wife always stayed in the kitchen or in the courtyard. He rarely found her in the living room when he visited. It was only in few occasions he had the chance to talk to her. His subject matter, though, needed somebody he spontaneously articulated his feelings to.

Uncle Khamis walked into the house after he parked his bicycle in the yard.

'Anwar', he called from the entrance, 'good to see you'.

'How are you, Uncle Khamis?' he said, shaking hands with him.

'Are they bringing any tea?' he asked.

'Yeah, it is coming', Anwar responded.

'Do you have an idea of what is going on?' Khamis asked as he entered the living room.

'No, I have been to the mosque and walked my way to the house', Anwar responded.

'The military fraction of the rebel returnees have incorporated most of the militia in town. The advantage for the militia is getting ammunitions. Since the *liwa* had banned allocating any militia any ammunition years back, it is feared they were being sneaked out of town. Now they are getting it from the defected rebels. Do you see the misperception?' Khamis asked.

'The war itself is shaped to serve no gain. That's why what the people say should be prevalently rational. Creating militias would make the national armed force an incompetent institution. The question becomes, as the main armed force, what do we do?' Anwar replied.

'Given the situation, the army should give equivalent ratios for all ethnicities. Otherwise, they make their separate crews, and the whole country is now in chaos', Khamis responded. 'Before I left town, I heard Wau Market closed early. Living in this town for this long, this is not a promising update. The unfolding of what created the divides is unleashing the tensions', he said. 'Are you in good terms with the *liwa*?' he asked Anwar.

'The problem with our leaders, they put proficient information to the side and seek to dilute their fears with rumours. I don't know if he takes whatever he is advised with reciprocal importance', Anwar replied.

'Be careful, Anwar, I have to caution you. In this war, sadly, everywhere had been a front line', he said with a sense of apprehension.

Sarah walked in with the tea. Khamis sat there, watching how Anwar was looking at her pouring the tea and realised what that meant. When she left the room, he began to talk. 'Sarah', Khamis started. 'I raised her to be a diligent girl. We need to teach girls that they are valued members of our societies. Education is key to eradicating many negative cultural inconveniences. She likes school. That's why I took care of her education', Khamis said. 'She is very young', Khamis continued thoughtfully.

Anwar was quiet; he perceived where Sarah got her desire to persist in her defined path. That was moving.

The days that followed were packed with events eliciting stories that induced frictions between mere civilians and armed militias. The stories were increasing in frequencies and intensifying every single day. He had grown very close to *naqib* Santino who was under great pressure being the stores person in the garrison. It was always challenging dealing with the demands of the different army fractions.

That morning he walked from his lodge to the store in the break of dawn. He found Abdel Azeem and Santino arguing fiercely.

'It's under your responsibility to find out what happened!' Abdel Azeem yelled.

'It's all because of your stupid fugitives. You counted on them more than everybody!' Santino yelled back.

'Are you taking sides with the rebels?' Adel Azeem asked him.

'You are the rebel now since it's your men who left the town'.

A team of armed men had left town. They happened to be close to the commander in chief in town. How that escaped his perception was mesmerising. He was there at the mercy of *naqib Santino*; now Anwar happened to learn of what had happened.

Both men were stunned to see a figure of a third character in their quarrel. Anwar stood mortified; how could he step away? 'Who is there?' *liwa* Abdel Azeem asked anxiously.

'Calm down, that must be Anwar', he said, striding slowly to the figure standing. And who on earth could that be? It was him, indeed, Anwar. They were all silent.

'Well, Anwar', *liwa* Abdel Azeem started, 'some of our intimates defected with their ammunitions. If there is anybody responsible, that would be myself'. He paused and took a deep breath. 'I ask your concealment, I mean both of you'. He saluted both men and exited.

Anwar was stunned at how this man had transformed since he first encountered him. That unruffled man brought to surface the need to connote that, eventually, there will be a need when everyone's role becomes effective. Even silence matters. That morning the aggressive, controlling, and pessimistic character of Abdel Azeem departed. He walked into humbleness. Or rather, the days that unfolded demanded that he becomes so.

By the end of February 1998, the entire party of the peace agreement defected from Wau town. Fear impelled thousands of civilians to leave their residences, walking into the bushes. What was left behind was a construction of a new divide in the town's societal fabric. The hit was strong. All their forces reversed to the main stations. From Nazareth, their allocated bunch reversed to protect the main garrison. That night he sneaked with Maher on a patrolling tanker all the way to Khamis's house. It was only the two of them on a tanker beside an empty house. There was no one inside the house. He sat by the steps, shading vicious tears. It was as if a precious part of him had been whipped in the haze of war. In war, everybody loses.

Maher was uneasy at Anwar's delay inside the house. He got off the car and found him sitting on the steps. 'Is she dead?' he asked.

Anwar looked at him. 'What do you mean?' he asked angrily.

'Then why are you crying like that?' Maher responded.

'What would be the direction of their exit?' he asked.

'Heah? Are you crazy? Even the army can't get to that side now. You and I can't do that. Let's return!' Maher yelled and walked out of the house.

He walked out of the patio, and they climbed the car. 'We have to take a different path back, or else, we will be lost like Sarah', Maher said mockingly

'You know what? You have always been a coward. Why did you even join the military?' Anwar yelled at him.

'Don't blame me for your failure. Why didn't you make your moves on her?' Maher asked. Anwar was quiet. 'Or you did?'

'Stop being dumb. I was going to propose', Anwar answered.

'Who told you Southerners marry? They steal and pay forfeits instead of dowry', Maher responded.

'Well, I love this girl!' Anwar yelled.

'Hehehe, my friend, you are crazy. Firstly, I am the one who took you to Khamis's house, and when you found your woman, you went behind me to Amu Mahdi to get things started', Maher said.

'I was', Anwar started.

'Shut up! Let me finish. When I first met Sarah, she used to walk bare feet, and boys used to mock her. She never bothered, I figured she was different. You think I could be at fault in the process? Second to that, you don't tell a woman you love her until you get a hold of her. Hey, wait, wait', Maher said.

'What?' Anwar asked.

'I see another patrol in the distance, they have stopped. What do we do?' said Maher.

'This is what I was saying, you are a coward. Let's drive there and talk to them', said Anwar.

'Salam aliekum', Anwar said, leaning forward from the passenger seat.

'Salam aliekum', said the man in the other patrol. 'What are you doing in this side of town?'

'Well, he was trying to rescue his fiancée', Maher said hesitantly.

'I have very close people here, and I figured they might need me. I arrived late', Anwar responded.

'There are two possibilities: Either they have left town and they might be in Kawagena by now or they went to the side of the Fertiet, most of whom have also defected. Whichever way, I advise that you be patient. The following days are going to be chaotic', said the man in the other patrol.

'Thank you, sir', Anwar replied.

They drove off.

'You know who the real coward is?' Maher asked.

'Who?' Anwar asked.

'The man who loses the woman of his dreams. Oh, mister dreamer. As for me, Maher, I am just a coward. You know, this town had been drifted as such so many times, you would think this is the end of the world, but soon you don't know where they come from, you see the Southerners back in their places', Maher said. Anwar looked away to the other side. To him, that particular drifting in time was far from over.

They returned to their barracks in the vague gloominess of that night. They parked at the same time as more heavy gunshots were heard around. He went to his lodging, laid on his belly, feeling his heart pumping like a mill. His muscles froze. The gunshots were not loud; his plight was louder.

'Anwar', a voice called him. It was the commander in chief, *liwa* Abdel Azeem. 'Have you been looking for Khamis and his family?' He was quiet. 'Answer me!' he yelled. 'Do you know that Khamis was a strong voice of opposition? The men who defected before the clash were some of his supporters. Anyway, our sources say some families have arrived Kawagena more than 20 miles away. They might be amongst them. I feel remorseful. I just wish saying sorry could be a resolution. Now get out of here. We are going to be moving together'.

The rainy season of 1998 was one that would go down in the records of the guardians of the town's seasons as one that dripped tears, for the dead and the living alike. Flashing thunders coupled shelling lights as if man's insanity was contesting natural incidences. The ground was soaked with the ruins where a rich heritage of tenacious dialogues and inclusivity was gaining thrust. There was a desperate reverence for the slightest potential for amity. And no, things didn't get back to how they were prior to the battle. Anwar had been to Bo Bridge. It was a front line of men. Nonetheless, Wau combat precinct was where everything about his hard-earned journey had dwelled. The defection in the town was a disadvantage to an intensely perceived aspiration. He suffered the rapture of comfort, and more than ever, the recognition that love was the rectifying power to every wound became an audacious pursuit.

For the rest of his stay in Wau and, indeed, his military duty, he had been a very close confidant of *liwa* Abdel Azeem and *naqib* Santino. They had known the complexity and deterioration of the events. It was a sharp decline that was counteracted through military manoeuvres.

KHARTOUM CITY

On 9 January 2005, Sudan stood between the assortments of individual stories, of journeys unheard of and of dreams that subsisted to silence firearms. For once, in a span of decades of the conflicts, in the face of an entire generation, the resolve was demonstrated in the benevolence to overcome. Numerous public departments were convened to address and amend the particulars of the peace accord. Khartoum City was the fundamental location in the story of the making of Sudan.

The First Sergeant, Anwar Fareed arrived Khartoum City in the mid of the winter season, by late 2004. His family had always instilled in him the potency to perusing a just cause. Their home was a cradle for the voiceless. The house was constructed at a time when a stone throw would delineate the contours of a property. Tradition dictates that the inlay would eventually develop into layers of an intergenerational-built dwellings. He was of the second generation. Given his single status, that meant empty spaces engrossed their estate.

The gate of their house was a heavy metallic double-sided painted jade door. On top was mosaic braces linked to spiral wires encircling the fence. It opened to a vast square contoured by lines of fences, ornamented entrances and fine passages into the neighbourhood. He walked out of the door not knowing where to from hither. He followed the path beside the open domain, where the winter breeze was rigid and parched, where dust shovel in the mirage of a detached reminiscences of his younger self. His subsequent intension became to find a *raksha*.

'Where to?' the driver asked.

'Dokan al harami', he responded and climbed the *raksha*. They reached in few minutes. He paid his fare and walked to the shop. 'Salam aleikum', Anwar called.

'Ohh, Anwar, your feet are cool. You brought peace with your arrival', Tariq, the shop owner, said from behind his counter in the canteen. He embraced him with a hug. 'I was away last week when you arrived. I was visiting our relatives in the village. There has been a funeral', he responded.

'My condolences', Anwar responded.

Tariq came out to where the beans was being cooked on a round aluminium pot placed over a faintly glowing charcoal stove. He dispensed the broiled beans into a flat tray-like plate with dressing salads. The bread was inside a sack on a four-legged table towering the cooking stove beside it. He went and collected a bunch without counting. 'How much is a piece?' he asked.

'Take what would satisfy you', Tariq responded.

'How much all together?' Anwar asked.

'This is for your service. Hope you get rewarded properly', he responded.

'Haa, Tariq, thank you. This breakfast will do', he responded. He had been going to that shop for as long as he his memory could recall. He had built his youthful self around the relishes of cooked *flavia*, popularly known as *fool masry* from the shop. That shop had a distinct catering of the *fool masry*. The cuisine was not that just a meal. It was a major fare for the students, the hardworking middle- and low-class citizens, the labourers, and the displaced. It is the meal of the meek. It had a sweltering nostalgia that commanded a discourse to an uprise.

He collected the tray and bread, holding them to the front, got another *raksha* to the house. Going to the kitchen side, he found his family was making a home-prepared meal.

'Anwar? For whom is the meal being prepared?' the maid asked him.

'Make me the fool, I need to go to the office right away', he responded.

He sat in the living room, turned on the TV where the broadcast was a discussion on what was anticipated of the peace arrival. He could not grasp a point from what was going on. Suddenly, fluently speaking representee pronounced affiliations to the movements. The foremost concern at the time was the outcome of an imminent referendum.

After relishing his hunger, he dashed on the eroded sands of the desert, walking along the outline of their borough a block away to a main road where the bus stops. He caught a bus to town. Everyone was either drawn to a newspaper or attuned to the broadcast that was sounding loud from the ceiling. Khartoum in winter had a subtle rapidity, unlike summertime, when passengers catch the bus and pour their annoyance along the journey. It was a drive absorbed in the anecdote of a defining interval in the course of the entire nation. At 10:00 a.m., the streets were not congested. Buses drove in the bright heat of the winter sun.

He arrived at the Qaida in town. The news of his bearings haven't stopped arriving the head offices of the armed intelligence in the capital city. Not knowing what the emphasis of his meeting at the main office would involve, comment his case to God, he knew one thing: He was never moved by repulsive, apprehensive sentiments anymore. He was moved by questions without answers, by evidence and casualties, by the will to reverse any built indignations; though strangely, he can't identify what his next steps would be. He had lost charisma and indecency; he walked heavy-hearted, not ever intending to initiate any conversation until asked to do so. He met *Liwa* Salih, a very flexible, friendly personality. They greeted with hugs. He was welcomed to his office with an admired significance. They had a conversation of how he was going to be transitioned to return to civil life. Nothing was mentioned about his controversies in Wau.

As if a whole segment of his journey had been liquidated. He had wanted the specifics to account in the whole story. Not as a single narrative but as part of an inclusive anecdote in the country's extensive ache to peace.

He walked, tottering beside the lane, and stopped to cross the rail line. He looked across the street, and there were taxis beside a diagonal road that leads to the main city square. Standing by the road for a chance to cross the street, he felt the spell of lost ambitions and a dive into an indefinite path, where anything was possible, even failure. The winter sun was scorching on his head as he crossed the streets with dashed vigour.

Liwa Salih had linked him to a team working with the internally displaced encampments. Having boldly expressed how he related to the plight of the Southerners, that was considered a closure to his unfinished endeavours. To attend to them, he would create an authentic connotation, where the predicaments on the disadvantaged could be framed in the conversations of the country's journey in an interim period to a significant decision. For the Southern people, the decision to autonomy was an insight to who they are as a people, the accrual of their voyage across the vast land named after an ancient people. They are intwined to that heritage of the people called Sudanese, the blacks, a question that had been pondered over every discourse, be it civil, political, and armed all together.

He went to meet Hassan Zarooq in one of the internally displaced residence offices in Omdurman. He had to take a taxi for the trip. It was more than an hour drive from home into the heart of the desert; where the winter sun was blistering with twinkling mirage, where desert winds shovel dust like rising ghosts, where the thirst for water like the thirst for the arms of a lover was never quenched, no matter what amounts of fluids he drank.

'Are we ever going to arrive?' he asked the taxi driver.

The taxi was so compact; though empty, he had to take the back seat to have enough room to stretch his legs. It was the smallest taxi he had ridden. The driver, sweating as if he was ploughing and not driving a motor vehicle, looked at him from the rear-view mirror.

'They called the place "the devil's head". You can just imagine how far that could be'.

He was totally uncooperative. 'I don't usually drive people here before taking my fare', he continued.

'I get you', Anwar responded.

They arrived to some sparse clusters of mud builds. The walls, the single rooms, the roofs, and the ground all looked the same. Some were sheltered in the entrances by sack sheds. The place was scarily empty. *Where are the inhabitants?* he thought. It was in the middle of nowhere. He could see the disorganised one-room builds one after the other, like cubic dunes of the desert. Gosh, he became thirsty again. The breeze smelt hay and dung.

'There are your people', the taxi driver responded, pointing to a very wide shed beside a stretched borough.

He took a deep sigh, knowing that any other word to his escorting fellow would not lead anywhere.

'Ahlan Anwar?' a young man almost his age got up and greeted him. 'I am Shogi, the assistant of the chief', he said.

He greeted him, and there was a team playing dominoes by the side of a small canteen. Everything in the place looked parched and too humble.

'Why did they send you over here?' another elderly man asked as he approached them.

'How are you? I am FazlullahDeng, one of the chiefsof the area'. He seemed to be unenthusiastic with his coming. 'You might need to come another time to meet Hassan Zarooq. He is not here today'.

Anwar did not know where to begin. He would share the same level of sentiments. Looking at their situation and returning himself from where circumstances were not in better conditions, he understood.

'I also needed to meet you', he responded.

'Ha, okay, *tamam*,' they responded happily.

There existed a plight of a lifetime. They had lived at the edge of the desert for decades in daring expectations. Sitting ashy in the scorching blast of the winter sun year after year, a lifetime went by day in and day out in contemplative expectations. Peace coming was the utmost aspired ordeal of a lifetime. Until it arrived, just like reaching a cliff, there was an acute edge to it. Any direction from there was costly.

Anwar had a genuine sense of connection and knew where to begin. Expressing his intention to meet them first, though accidentally, made them feel of value in his sight. Coming from the South made him someone they wanted to listen to.

'Did you get yourself a wife from there?' Shogi asked.

'The *anya-nya* have stolen the girl I was going to marry seven years ago, and I decided not to marry', he responded.

'Are you serious? Just tell me her family, and I will bring her back to you'.

'No, don't tell Shogi', the chief said. 'He will take her for himself. He already has two who are even very young'.

'You just pay me some cows, and I will let her go', Shogi responded jokingly. 'My friend, women don't have a tribe', he continued. 'If you love her, we will bring her back to you. Now the borders are open. Why would somebody else take your place?'

At the mention of the marriage, many more people came to hear what the story of the stolen girl was. They stood beside them, listening and laughing at the interesting conversation. It's a definite calling, marrying the girl you love. You have to summon the tactics of the entire family and friends to support you to get her. Shogi seemed to be amongst those who win; evidently, he has two women already. He clapped his hand, rubbing them together, and responded, 'I am ready when you are'. That seemed to be an exciting subject.

'Okay, now, Anwar, you have come and seen our place, and you should come again when Hassan is available so we can meet', the chief interrupted as evening was approaching. 'You have to return now, Anwar, soon the place will be full of people returning from the city, and you will not know how to find your way back'.

To their astonishment, Anwar returned the next day; this time he arrived on a back of a passenger Hilux. It was around mid-morning; the winter sun was blazing hot. The white nylon sacks covering the huts reflected bright and gleaming rays over the neighbourhood. The chief and Hassan were there under the same shed, having tea. 'Come and sit here, Anwar'. The chief got up and gave him his chair. 'This is Anwar, the man I talked to you about', the chief said to Hassan.

'I am Hassan Zarooq', Hassan responded. 'I got a message about your coming. Yesterday I was not here. Today we see who we can find to start working with'.

'Adarop, bring more tea please', Hassan called to the shop owner who was called Abu-Amna. Adarop is a nickname of a man from the east of the county where Abu-Amna comes from. There exist a popular tradition of tea catering, where a golden teakettle is tied to a charcoal stove and carried around by the merchant. He had that in his shop. The tea neither runs out of taste nor gets cold. They drank the morning tea, pondering what would be their next step be.

'I will go and call Helen', Hassan said. 'She is the women representative, so they won't dispute our decisions'. He walked to the middle of the unconstructed path to a house not far from the shop.

'Ya, Helen, Helen', Hassan called from the gate. They could hear him from the distance.

From an aperture in her build, Helen heard the voice and was awaken by the calling of her name, lifting herself off the bed, bent to exit the slot opening of her shanty house. Outside, the clay plastered yard was smearing from the torrid heat. A blurred stature was standing in front of her hut. She could barely identify who that was. Annoyed, she said, 'Aye, who are you? And why did you wake me up?'

'It is breakfast time, my sister, why are you even still sleeping?' the person said. She recognised his voice. It was Hassan. He was one of the neighbourhood committee members, and for some reason, he was one of the caring people she met. She rubbed her eyes to see better but couldn't. She had grown frail over the series of days spent with no proper sustenance. 'Well', Hassan continued so not to keep her longer as he realised her posture. 'I came to tell you that the chief said some people will come to talk to us about the return program, and we will meet them at the shed near the marketplace'.

Helen opened her eyes. She has been waiting for that moment. When the drought struck their fields almost 20 years ago, the men left one after the other. They never returned, and nothing was heard from them since. She left the village seven years later to seek decent earnings. As she became the breadwinner, she had to look in surrounding areas as there were no prospects for recovery in the village. The search took her further and further away from home. Thousands of miles behind, she left her children to the guardians of the clan. It wasn't meant to take that long. It was a trip to work on the nearby scheme for a season and return. But there she was, living at the outskirt of the city for almost a decade, holding on to the hope of seeing her children and village again.

She looked at Hassan with disbelief. No word uttered. Her thoughts took her to her village. Her children are now grown-up. She won't even recognise them. How would she justify her long absence? The news she received whilst away was that her departure was not accepted. As a woman, she had no right to independent choices. But she left, against all expectations. Over the years, she pressed hard to the limits of her aptitude with the hope of a fulfilling reward on her return. But there she was, her face sunken with misery over the dreadful years. She thought to herself, after so long, at least her dream of meeting her children again was becoming a reality. 'You know what', she said, 'I will come'.

AMU ABUANJA

Amu Salim Abuanja, a left-wing political columnist, learnt of a soldier from the Southern divisions called Anwar Fareed who had recently return to Khartoum. He wanted to reinforce his criticism with more facts, so he sought to hear from him the stories the government media was not telling. Through indirect friendship ties, he got to have Anwar visit him in his home office, in a very quiet district of Omdurman, not far from the city centre. Almorada, meaning 'the anchorage', is one of the intrinsic Sudanese districts from chronical times, a countenance of the emergence of an authentic Sudanese refinement, one of the district names in the making of the history of Sudanese urban civilisation. It evolved from a shipping station during the Mahadia movement in the late 19th century to an overwhelmingly vibrant district at the time Anwar was visiting. Even so, the simple native imprints can be detected as one moves through the locale. The historic southern gate of Omdurman subsisted as a monument of valour and ancient civilisation.

He entered a hall-like room with a low ceiling that his head could almost touch the roof. All he could see were piles of worn-out newspapers all over the floor. A line of antique shelves stood on one side with rusted books. There was a four-sided window on the far end of the wall with one quarter opening to where the sun beamed into the room. He could see smoke ascending in a spiralling line in the beam light out of the window.

'Come and sit', said a voice from beside a pile of mounted papers. He was sitting on an antique upholstered couch. He had one hand on the armchair and was holding a burning cigarette with the smoke rolling into the air. The room was so cold. The flour was sedimented with bricks. A sophisticated rug was positioned in the curvature of a siting area on which was a coffee table.

He sat without handshake. 'How can we work together?' Abuanja asked him.

'What?' Anwar asked, pretty bewildered at how far his voice had reached. 'These people don't have much now', he continued. 'They were left between hard choices, leaving their leadership or allowing the Southerners to decide for self-determination. That made them acquiescent to critical views'.

'I am not so much into politics, except for few involvements during my student life', Anwar said.

'Somebody with your pace of contribution should aim far. You need an ideological understanding of the political arena', he said, leaning to the coffee table and knocking the ash off the burning cigarette. He has been holding the cigarette and talking as the smoke kept meandering in the room. They were quiet. It was clear that Abuanja sees in Anwar not just someone to correspond with, but rather a new voice for the coming time.

'Cigarettes?' he asked.

'I decided to quit. Tea, please', Anwar responded.

'Good, I haven't had my tea since they brought it. I have been totally alienated, you know. My best friends are my papers now. My wife talks to me from the distance. I don't blame her, there is a cost to everything. And this is one of the things you get for telling the truth'. He took a deep breath and walked to a side table where the tea thermos was put. It was then that Anwar had seen his full figure. He had a small stature. His unshaved beard gave him a giant feature.

He returned to their seats with the teacups. 'Married or engaged?' he asked.

'Nnmmm', Anwar murmured.

'So you are the one who is in love with a *junubia*? That was what I suspected. So here, I got in front of me the prince of Sudan'. He looked at Anwar, gazing above his thick glasses, and said, 'You never stopped impressing me'.

'Haj', Anwar responded with a very deep sigh. In a way, he was giving him his due status as an uncle.

'Look, I tell you this, son, just put your best efforts forward, you don't know where you would get to. Wherever you get to, let it be worth your efforts'.

Gradually, Anwar got used to the cold, foggy compact chamber of Abuanja's home office. They had a convoluted conversation of how the situation was superficially pushing the Southerners to opt for secession. In his solitary navigation in the world of articulating critical pronouncements, Abuanja had shrunk to the confinement of his man's cave. That day he began another journey.

Together with Abuanja, they began a series of findings in the anecdotes of history of how Sudan evolved. One of the major redress to history was the question of who the Sudanese were, a parameter that required a willingness to correct what was left unattended in the populace discourse. There was a name to the character of their finding.

'Allow me to call him the man of Sennar', Abuanja said to Anwar.

'Very captivating', Anwar said. 'I picture him as a valiant who was born with a definite calling to restore all lost heritage of his people's domain'.

'Anwar', Abuanja said, looking from above his glasses, 'I see that man around here. I picture him as a dignified and civilised individual with traditions and norms, though he was betrayed in the records of the centralised objective brainstorming'.

'Now the change of tide meant that every account deserved the permission to be stated as history had dictated, not as counterfeited to fit a particular propaganda', Anwar responded.

'How did you manage with the government there in Wau?' he asked.

'I thought I would be staying in a locked place. It wasn't so. What I had observed was that, at some point, the populace would erupt from the bursting of hurts and contempt of their compliance', Anwar responded.

They were quite for a while, so immersed in their appraisals. That observation was a conclusion that would evidently shift populous rationale and influence the course of the status quo. Not that it wasn't known, but it was not acknowledged as it was.

Abuanja leaned forward, moved his thick glasses from his face, and continued talking. 'Sudan existed for more than four centuries with the same ethnic assortments. Those who assumed power had imperfectly used this rich heritage in their tenacious pursuit'.

Anwar walked out of the complex monumental homes of Abuanja's neighbourhood. It was travelling into past civilisation. He got a taxi to cross the river back to his house. As they passed, the smell of the fish market by the anchorage swayed his attention. 'What should be done about this pungent smell?'

Astonished by the question, the driver looked from his rear-view mirror at the person asking the question and wondered if the passenger was talking to him or to himself. Anwar was looking out through the glass window. 'Nothing', he responded. They kept on moving on the road.

When he arrived in his neighbourhood it was dawning already, the A'azan started loud enough to deafen the sounds of the demons of defeat. He walked to the mosque for his first prayer of the day. Most of the attendees were elderly. After they finished, the imam called him, 'Anwar, are you all right, my son?'

'Thanks be to God', he responded and walked to the gate back home. They were sensing that something was bothering him. The reality was the whole country was undergoing a rapid transformation. Why would Anwar be that excessively worried was the concern. In the series of following months, that morning prayer was the last time he had been seen in the mosque. He found a hidden beer merchant with whom he started an affair and spent most of his service compensation expense until he was broke.

Anwar would visit Amu Abuanja late in the evenings, and they would work through the night reading what had been published in the editorials and speculating what that could do in the approaching mess. A friend of Amu Abuanja suggested for him to join the local government, in which he would have the chance to have a distinct opinion and earn a decent income. That, though, was a shift too quick for his sickening soul. He was better off drunk, meeting with Amu Abuanja, at the displaced camps, or sleeping at home. He chose to elude to be totally concealed off the recounting of the pains of history. It was an interval of a much-needed healing.

One very late night, Anwar turned to his drinking place to find it fully occupied by new faces. He was no longer a required guest. He walked shaky on the street and couldn't finish his route walking, so he got onto a *raksha* to get to his place. Just close to home, he couldn't find his wallet. They returned along the same route in case it had fallen along the way. It was nowhere to be found.

'Can you go back to the house you were in to search there?' the *raksha* boy asked him.

'No, no, I can't go back there', he responded.

Worried about his fare, the boy asked, 'Why not? You are just looking for your wallet'.

'I tell you this . . .' Anwar went on getting off the *raksha* and hardly standing. 'I-I will return to the station tomorrow morning to pay you. What's your name and number?'

'You know what', he said very annoyed, 'get in the *raksha*'.

He got in happily, and off the *raksha* went, only to stop by a police station. They found the station packed inside by late night incidences, and Anwar refused to get off. Entering the station drunk meant lashes and a fine. The guard by the gate approached them to find out what was going on.

'What is going on, boy?' he asked with a very course tone.

'He won't pay me', he said angrily.

'Why don't you pay him? Can you get out of the *raksha*?'

'I can't, *janabu*. I promised to pay him, if this will do', Anwar responded from under the drapes of the *raksha*.

'That won't work. Can I have your ID, please?' the police said.

'It is lost in my wallet', he responded.

'Your name, please', the police said.

'Anwar Fareed, *janabu*', he responded from under the *raksha*.

'Oh, Anwar? Do you know Taher?' the police asked him.

'Was he in the army?' he asked.

'Yes, from Wau', the police responded.

'I know him', he said.

'He lives in our neighbourhood. He told me a story about Anwar Fareed. He also told me you lived around here. I am now on duty. Otherwise, I would take you to him. Can you come tomorrow in the afternoon?' he asked.

'Okay', Anwar responded.

'I am Jalab Talib. You will be finding me sitting by the gate', he said. 'Hey, boy, here is your fare', he said, pulling some cash from his pocket to the raksha driver. 'Is it even now?' he asked.

'It is', the boy responded.

They drove very quietly in the empty tarmac boulevard to his place. The boy was quiet, which made him wonder. As he got off the *raksha*, the boy called him with his name, 'Anwar'. He turned to him to find out what was more. 'Have you been to the South?' he asked.

'Yes, I was in the South. Why do you ask?'

'I lost my eldest brother in the South', he responded. 'Take some of the fare for your transport tomorrow', he said, giving him 50 pounds.

'You know what, this *raksha* ride was a total challenge. Did you tell the police I am drunk?' he asked.

'He didn't ask me', he responded. They slapped their hands, and the *raksha* drove off.

Anwar entered the house wondering what the hell he was thinking. He felt totally minimised in the inevitable greatness of his calling. He went to where the bed was set out in the patio and lay down to only wake in midday.

When he woke, the sun was too bright overhead, it dimmed his sight. He had to stand for a little whilebeside the bed, absorbing its warmth in the rigid wind of the desert. Dressed in a smart casual, he walked out of the gate, recaptured his aptitude, and like the day, he bought the fool for breakfast, never knowing to hither would the path take him. He had only the 50 pounds at his possession. That day the pound had a profound value in his sight. That was the amount that would reverse a single yet a crucial story in the merger of all narratives and, indeed, the course of his lifetime.

He got on a minibus to save the change for his return home. To his amazement, the police officer was in waiting by the gate. Jalab was eager to connect him with Taher. He heard the story of an army internee who went to the South, challenged the structure in the military barracks with very simple impulsiveness. Later he went to one of the most confounding zones of war and returned. Meeting him in person was a remarkable encounter.

Anwar was fascinated by how Taher had described him to his friends. They have been in so much of the trials of the occurrences of the town and never seemed to be in good terms. He was eager to meet Taher again. All his grudges have been laid off the path of return to civility.

They arrived in AbuAdam after a ride on a private shuttle from Shaabi Police Station. They got off beside a house, the only house standing, suspended in an empty block. That seemed to be a likely place for Taher. Jalab knocked on the door. To their good coincidence, Taher was in the house, watering his newly flattened yard. The door was opened by a presumably younger Taher. He was his father's imprint.

'What a surprise!' he shouted from where he was standing, holding his hose. 'Anwar in person! I was telling your story when I invited some friends for dinner the other day'.

'Oh really, you never stopped talking about me even here?' Anwar responded jokingly.

They were seated where the crust was steady. The setting sun had a superb scenery over distant flat roofs of the desert-style constructions. The wind blew cold over the smearing dispatching heat off the ground. Another vast patio suspended the house marked by brick fence.

'Alf hamdila ala salma', Taher said.

'Taher, I knew I would find Anwar. I am a detective after all', Jalab said.

'They should upgrade you', Taher said. 'So how did you two meet?'

'This is another story', Anwar responded.

'You are never out of captivating stories', Taher responded. 'Is it another lover?'

'No, there is only one love. Now I am just a simple citizen with no attached title', he responded.

'You had a wonderful stay in Wau, you even looked happier there with all your confusions. You should do what pleases your heart. Maybe she will return'.

'Most families had to leave town out of fear. But I stayed when you moved to Khartoum. I met many people who had returned. She got married, that was what I heard'.

'She will probably return if she felt the same way towards you. A woman can fight the entire tribe for her man. She is a kind of woman who could do that', Taher said.

'You did good getting yourself this plot', Anwar said.

'I put all my recompense into this to reward my wife, or otherwise, she will not be happy with me', Taher said.

'Get yourself a place in AbuAdam here, it is all empty', Jalab said. 'Then go back to the South and bring her over here'.

'She is nowhere to be found', Anwar responded.

'You know what you need to do? Get yourself a good job, make good money, and go to the South again. Look for her and bring her before they divide the country', Jalab said.

'Is that what is going to happen?' Taher said.

'It is evident. You, the *jalaba*, have obstructed every opportunity. Now the peripheries are going one after the other', Jalab responded.

'Are you in support of that, Jalab?' Anwar asked.

'The situation will turn around at some point', Jalab said. 'The Southerners have not worked well in building strong coherence themselves. They have so much to do with regard to social justice and livelihood facilities. I even know people who went there and have returned already'.

'I don't have to support or not. I sit on the gate of a police station and watch every day how the law had separated them. This is just one example. What did your lover tell you, Anwar?'

'Haa, she-she has an indomitable vigour. I would actually encourage her and concede to her decision, though, I would state my viewpoint', Anwar responded.

'You love the girl, Anwar?' Jalab asked. 'Was that why you were drunk?' As an officer, he had realised that, but his intuition told him to not interrogate since there was no offence.

'Now you made me feel like a complete failure', Anwar responded.

Anwar arrived at the house that night with an altered attitude. To him, there was no more reason for regression. He was tremendously inspired by the simple encounters with the *raksha* boy, the police officer, and of course, Taher. How wherever he had been throughout his stay in Khartoum, the narratives of his time in Wau haven't missed his insights in the major discourse. His journey became worth accomplishing, the token for him was never giving up.

He decided to return to Wau to search for Sarah to earn back the love of the girl he had watched grow and whose courage he had admired. He intended to prevail for his country and procure the desire to overcome the plights of war. He had already spent ttwo years in delusion, so why wouldn't he? He stood in the empty yard of his father's estate and assembled his vigour to allow no withdrawal from his virtuous intent. For the remaining months of the year, he began to prepare for the return to Wau again.

MEETING SARAH AGAIN

O n 1 December 2008, Anwar arrived at Wau. That day the breeze was stiff and so cold. However, he was heavily perspiring from to his relentless apprehension and redundance of the evident complexity of his second mission in town; his individual quest for meaning in life. He called Maher from the airport to tell him he arrived. Though surprised, Maher knew Anwar would return at some point.

'Too soon', Maher said, hugging his good old friend.

'It is called welcome back, not too soon. It has been four rough years already', Anwar said, hugging him back.

'You know what, you are better here. Why would you even return for good? Who asked you to leave?' Maher asked as they walked to the car.

'You know what, you are just the same—a very free spirit. And you seem to be enjoying civil life', Anwar said when they got into the car.

He just looked at him without saying anything. They drove the same road where the car turned towards the corridor of the invincible landscapes, mounting monuments, and the characteristic motions of Wau municipality. The red soil embraced the blondness of the dry grasses in a symmetrical decent expanse. Though he was feeling a different compulsion at the time, he felt he belonged again. The scenery was nostalgic. He felt the chills of what nature bestowed moaned beneath his hankering drive to finish that which would console his tenor.

'Welcome home', Maher said from beside him, realising how drawn away Anwar was. 'Do you remember that night?' Maher asked.

'Don't remind me, eeshsh', Anwar replied with a very deep sigh. 'Have you heard about her?'

'You just told me not to remind you, and no, I didn't', Maher responded.

The scenery intrigued candid reminiscences from the beginning of his encounter with the appealing sensation of meeting Sarah, his gazelle. This time he was a mere individual, a name like anybody at the crossroads of pivotal period of decision-making. He stayed with Maher near a market that he wasn't used to visiting during his first stay.

Sooq Jaw is a very popular market on one of the main roads in town, the Raga Road. Extending on both sides of the street, the market is a characteristic merger of home-grown and imported produces. The whole market is masked with ardent aromas of sweet fruit smells to pungent fermented cuisines. Echoes of pumping mills in the blowing winds and exhaustive motions of buying and selling made the market the busiest place in town. They passed by to collect some groceries and see Maher's textile shop. That was what he had established for his livelihood. He seemed to be enjoying his new vocation moving and chatting all over the place.

Taking off from the market, they drove only one block to get to Maher's neighbourhood. The house was basically within the suburbs of the marketplace, a well-decorated square covered with sand and flowering shrub lines surrounded by a fence of fine thatch straws. The house was two separate huts and a shed.

'You are very brilliant enough to decide to get yourself a wife and start a family soon after leaving the military', Anwar said to his friend as they got to rest under a very conveniently set reception.

'You mean, she got me', Maher said jokingly.

The reception place was a thatched shed shielded on opposite ends by the walls of two separate huts, whilst the rest was all straw, with the exception of the doorway. Anwar sat on a fine teak sofa, listening to nature's breath whispering from beneath the abundant frondescence of Maher's patio. The house was so simple and unruffled despite the intense haphazardness of the market. The direction of the noise seemed to bypass them.

As the days passed, in his distress over how his life had turned, Anwar began to find solace in the songs of Noor El Gailany, a popular artist at the time, one of his favourites. El Gailany's works were expressions that resonated with his squandered efforts and rebellion against daunting prejudices. The more he decided to conflict his sense of loss, the more he felt detached from his purpose. He went to Wau Market, to Amu Mahdi. Part of the township had dilapidated in just few years from the last time he had been there. Roofs stood tarnished as they were, but the brick walls were too worn out. Unlike the olden times, Wau Market was much populated. The drums of separation were on almost every broadcast. The perpetual provocation of the years of build indignation never ceased. He could hardly recognise anybody besides Amu Mahdi and Juma. Or maybe he was too absorbed in his personal chronicles of romantic encounters with Sarah. Everywhere seemed to remind him of her. The entire town was an epithet of how they met. 'Wow.'

'Anwar, my son, I thought you would be better over there', Amu Mahdi said after some extended greetings.

'You are very skinny', Juma said. 'That side of the country is not good with you'.

'You mean that mother country, Juma?' Anwar responded. 'Since there is already a new pound in town, then this is a new state'.

'Yes, this pound equals that pound', Juma responded happily. He is always happy where numbers work appropriately.

They had some tea as it was always the norm. This time the pleasant smell of mint did not match his disenchanted disposition. Even the tone in place was an appalling surge to the eventual approach of the secession in plan. In most public assemblies, the message was an obvious preference dictated by the residues of situations manoeuvred to match the worst of consequences.

In one of his tours, he met Ayom. Ayom had gained much weight and appeared years older so much that he hardly recognised him anymore.

'Comrade Anwar', he called out from a very fine car.

'It is you, Ayom', he responded. 'How come you are driving and I am not?' he asked jokingly. 'How is the situation?'

'It is clear, the country is dividing', Ayom responded.

'I see you have already made up your mind', Anwar said to him.

'You, the *jalaba*, have your share of things getting this far. You see, the towns in the South survived one colonial and mission works. Not many developments seen since then'.

'Have you done anything for things to help turn around?' Anwar asked.

'Hey, yeah, me, what? Here? This is a very harsh situation. Everybody is vicious, everybody is despondent, this is the rule of the forest. We are just observing', Ayom responded. 'You know how the saying goes, "The hyena raised its children". Now they made the country like the forest they have been to, and we became the hyena. There is so much of getting along that is needed in a place where the civilians are the majority'.

'And what could be the usual conditions?' Anwar asked.

'Usually, the armed forces make the absolute majority, that is how the situation was over there. Now the civilians have returned', Ayom responded.

In just a week's time, he had met most of his good friends, yet the weave of sorrow still painted his face as he aimlessly toured around the town for days. In one of his dire frustrated deliberations in seeking answers to where Sarah could be, Anwar thought of having a last tour in town with high anticipation of finding a clue. And as his feelings had indulged, he met Sarah beyond Jaw Market. He had not been to that side by himself before. Contrary to their first encounter, this time he was an ordinary civilian, not belonging to the status quo. And she, in his eyes, is still that gazelle. This time she was not by herself. Beside her were two very young fellas.

'You!' he said.

She gazed at him with dilated eyes. 'Anwar!' she called out with a sigh of relief.

'Yes, it is me'. He could see the misery hidden behind her pretty eyes.

Both were silent. There was so much of explanations required to digest.

'You left during the dispersal', she said.

'No, I did not. I stayed a couple of years more', he said. 'I searched for you, so much. I went to the house again and again, hoping you would return'.

Breathing hard, she said, 'I had to leave, you know. But I returned three years later'. She began to fight back her tears as she continued talking. 'Since I never saw you, I was terrified to ask. I convinced myself into believing that you were still alive', she said with a brittle sound.

'I am here as you can see', he said, taking a step towards her, breathing heavily, feeling every heartbeat. 'Are they yours?' he asked, looking at the boys standing by her side.

'Yes', she said.

'They have your eyes', he said, looking at them. 'Little champs, are you being good to her?' One of them nodded, and the other simply hid behind their mother's wide skirt.

He never wanted to accept that this is what it has come to be, never wanting to say goodbye. But he was too fragile to say more. With more deep breaths, he said, 'See you again then, God willing'.

She nodded, and both walked in opposite directions. He turned around to see her disappearing in the distance. He walked away heavy-hearted. As for his pursuit, it was not finished.

The streets seemed empty as he marched off to find Maher. He arrived at the house where he was staying with Maher, dashed through the gate to the direction of the shed.

'Maher, Maher', he called as he was entering the building. There was nobody there.

'Yes. Where have you been the whole day?' Maher responded from inside one of the huts.

'I have found Sarah today', he said cheerfully.

'You did? Why didn't you bring her to visit?' asked Maher.

'I need your help', he said.

'Why do you need my help now, ha? You know well that I am a coward', Maher said.

'She has kids', Anwar responded.

'Your kids?' Maher asked.

'Maher, it is not like what you are assuming', Anwar responded with a more serious tone.

'Then tell me everything so I can help. A woman with kids would be so much dowry to pay'.

'Maher, this is not a joke', again, he responded.

'Where is she staying?' Maher asked.

'I don't know', he said, getting himself a chair.

'I see you really love this woman'. He paused. 'Things have changed now. We are now on the other end of the social discord. We no longer have the authority to anything. If she was taken by one of the comrades, it is going to be hard'.

'That's why I need your help to find out'.

'Anwar, my life is here. I can't create any trouble. We can only find out where she is staying. If she is happy, then that is all', Maher responded.

'Not for me!' he yelled back.

'Calm down, my friend. This country is even going to separate. This is quite perceptible. Get off your romantic dreams, they are unrealistic for this time!' he yelled back.

Anwar looked at Maher like he was meeting him for the first time. As much as he had ridiculed his reasoning, that day he was the insane one, and Maher became the one with more rational discerning. 'Because it is too profound, I won't get off. This is my contentment. This town is my home, and she is my lover'.

'I see this is a real situation. Is that why you returned, Anwar?' Maher asked.

Anwar was quiet.

'Now where is she? Tell me, were you going to marry her like a princess? You were supposed to act according to the situation at the time and make a shortcut, even steal her. If she loved you back, then that is all there is', Maher responded.

'Anyway, there is time beyond this time, and there is a reason to believe that things will inverse to good times', he responded, fighting his tears.

'Hey, hey, hey, don't ever get back to being on the side of expectation, ever. Do you hear me?' Maher responded.

Though opposing his friend, Maher was moved by his being incapable of doing anything to his good old friend. He was very conscious and sensitive of the realities of what was evolving in the country. He had to be more careful, though, because his subsistence was exclusively in the town. He didn't make any plans to depart after returning to a civil life. It is obvious that Anwar has been transformed by his military experiences across the country. He could not be persuaded to think otherwise. When a man set his aptitude on a cause, it becomes a state of being or not being, either to accomplish or die trying to accomplish that which would bring the truest contentment. Anwar's one was far-reaching. He dares not to discourage anymore, though he can't solve the puzzle.

Another week passed. The year turned. Anwar walked from the informally modest suburbs of the town's societal timelines to a path adjacent to a vast extension of an inlay valley of orchard gardens. It is a major partition like an imperial garden with evergreen vegetations offering an imposing raw elegant culmination as he passed by. Every new year, the discreet landscape of the town owes so much courteousness. The rhythm of the town itself accommodates this natural frequency. Noticeably, the trees and vegetations below have grown in a beautiful disorderly manner, sending forth scents of pollen syrups and sweet vanilla smell of ripe barks. He walked the giant pathway towards the narrow bridge and off to the other side of town.

He had a steady climb on the ascending undulating crust of Sooq Hagr. Every marketplace seemed to be more crowded and louder than before. Every canteen sets its broadcast volume louder than its adjacent counterpart. If given the permission to vote, he would be bewildered. Knowing that nothing could alter how the turn of events have toughened people's perception, including himself; the recount of the damages to consciences and virtue are what needed individual intuitive rehabilitation to accommodate all the abrupt fluctuations in everyday life.

His soul was heavy with defeat; that time in history was a protuberance where every aspect of what life demanded conjugated. He felt his plight was deeper in soul. A malaria fever was no longer a challenge; neither a long-distance walk. That which rendered the time, the real challenge was what the inevitable decision would mean to his individual life, just pondering what he would say to convince Sarah. He would search the pathways and get to where she was. He had nothing to make up; he would come as blunt as he would.

The prospect of a new nation was more evident than ever. He could see that the South was not one narrative of armed involvements or the government against the rebels. His involvement as a militant was a segment of plenty narrations of complexities that had influenced the approaching outcome. Lost in his thoughts, he heard his name from the distance, 'Anwar, Anwar'. That was Ayom on his classic Toyota, driving over the rugged tarmac road. Like they say, 'The cars arrived before the roads'. 'Where to?' he yelled from the distance.

'Grinity!' Anwar yelled back.

'Let's go, I was going to pass by after visiting a project nearby. Are we going to comrade Santino?'

'Your language has totally changed, my friend. If I didn't know you before, I would say you were a rebel', Anwar said.

'This is what you have to do to get along here. Now your uncle Santino is in trouble because he seemed to be more loyal to previous orders and conducts himself as if one of the Northern officials. They are going to remove him', Ayom said.

'If what he does serves the new system, then that is what is important', Anwar said.

'Not everybody sees things that way, my friend', Ayom responded.

Without realising, he had arrived at his former residence in Grinity, where the handing-over process was effective. This time they needed permit to enter the premises. 'Stop. What are you here for?' a voice from a shuttle building at the gate called out. A different tone was in place. Thanks to Ayom, things were easier. The hustle was more, and the motions were intense. They drove calmly into the complex of the lodging and towards the storehouse.

'Anwar', that voice called him again from the distance. It was Naqib Santino. His voice still harbours the unchanged substantial affirmation that reminded him he meant something. The reunion brought to mind the first time they met. It was after separating a wrestle. There was more wrestling around to deal with. But this time the wrestle was one that was too big for him. There was no permission to endure; they had to pack up, hand over, and leave.

'I am going to hand over the store and move out of town', he started.

'Can't you remain for a little while? You are the one in charge', Anwar asked Santino in a way to encourage him.

'No, they wanted everything right away. Handing over is good for me'.

'It's not that you have a militia or something', Anwar responded.

'Even so, he could be suspected. This entire region is being suspected', Ayom said.

'You watch out being around in town these days', Santino said to them.

They bid farewell to Santino and took a drive over the flat hill landscape, where Ayom was building his house. 'This is my focus now', he said to Anwar.

'You seem to be doing good here then', Anwar responded.

'How about you? What have you done?' Ayom asked.

'I am here searching for a girl I was courting before the dispersal', Anwar responded.

'Oh, poor Anwar, don't tell me she is Khamis's daughter. I heard of the story that one of my friends was courting her. I suspected that to be you', Ayom asked.

'Do you have any idea where she is staying now?' he asked.

'She lives on the Fertiet side now. I will help you get there. You just have to be very careful. There have been so many troubles around over women lately', Ayom said.

'Just let me get to her, and I will find my way from there. I will be ready very late in the evening', Anwar said.

Ayom dropped Anwar to Maher's place and returned at dusk. It was one of the drives that assembled all his sought-for contentment. Silently, they traversed the resounding boulevards of straw-lined fences overarched by gigantic mango trees. Every yard happened to have its share of trees. Calm was the drive. Ayom was driving. He turned to Anwar. 'Why do think you need to get to her?'

Anwar was quiet. Feeling awkward, he tried to explain himself. Ayom continued, 'I mean, with all that is taking place and you could be returning to the North'.

'I don't have a precise answer, Ayom. I am coming from the North. I have also been to the front line with you, you remember?' Anwar said.

'We have been to Bo together', Ayom confirmed.

'And I ask myself, what is more satisfying in this life? Now I see you people here, and that confirms what I gather to be the answer. You are doing your best for the people you love the most'.

'I see', Ayom said, surrendering his argument.

They were almost out of town when they arrived at the place Sarah was staying. The buildings were more scattered, it was quieter, it was far-flung at the edge of the town. *She must be really unhappy to distance herself this much and move to this part of town,* Anwar thought.

They knocked a sturdy gate clearly made of crude barrels. The sound of the knock was as heavy as Anwar's heartbeat.

'Who is it?' she asked from the inside.

'It's Anwar. Open the door, Sarah', Anwar responded.

'Anwar, are you out of your mind? What are you doing here?' Sarah asked furiously from behind the gate.

'I will wait beside the car when you are ready', Ayom said, realising his presence would be awkward to the situation.

'Are you by yourself?' she asked as she opened the door.

He entered and closed the gate. The enclosure covered the entire block; the house itself was a concise rectangular building at the ingress.

'Are you living by yourself here?' he asked her. She was quite wondering what his question meant. 'Or is there somebody around?'

'Was that why you are coming at this time, to find a proof?' she asked.

'You can't be living in such a place', Anwar said.

'My place is not such a place, Anwar', she responded.

'At least let me have a seat', Anwar responded.

'Why are you here, Anwar?' she asked irritated.

'I am here for you', he responded. 'Why have you neglected how you felt towards me?'

'This is not a time for such a talk. I have a different life now', she responded.

'Can I have a seat?' he asked again.

'This is a different time, Anwar, and it is very harsh. You should know that better than me', she responded.

'For what I know, not much is for you here as much as not much is there for me on the other side', he said. 'People like us have to state their existence one way or another'.

'Anwar, you took a gun, and I didn't. I don't belong to your team either. The costs the Southern civilians have paid is enormous enough. They deserve to speak', she responded.

'I need you back in my life. There is much we can do together. You are a woman full of discernments, and my love for you had grown', he said, abruptly pulling her in his arms.

She was annoyed instead. 'Anwar, tell me, is this why you needed me in your life, to work against what is taking place?' she asked.

'No, dear'. He paused then continued, 'I crossed a massive distance to get you. The reason cannot only be to join against anything. It is simply called virtue'. He placed his forehead against her head, not wanting to accept that he has been defeated again. Years ago, the day Sarah left the town with her family, during the dispersal, another anecdote had been counterfeited in the order of fate. It was a barrier that had cost so much. For him, it had demanded too much resilience, and it had etched on his conscience time and again. All that he could do as a man was to allow her the respite of sentiments from the aches of desolation.

In silence, they drove the urban comrades, and away they went. When all the guns were put down, in the silence of amity, what does a gallant draw out of himself? As a soldier, Anwar could attest that the battle for love is an eventual pursuit and fiercer than that of a combat zone. It is a battle for repletion, when it's arrived to win, and only win becomes the absolute steadfastness. Their drive back to the house was quiet, aloof, diving in thoroughfares of secluded dreams. As for the days that followed, they were the toughest.

CROSSING THE SUSPENSE

T he reality of peace was that the everyday experiences were not reinforcing a path that predicted the accomplishment of many people's senses of individual contentment. That time was contrasting every prospect of a foreseeable coherence in considerate actions by the mere civilians. In the height of the political situations, civilians arrived at their home estates, finding the receptive communities in a state of unpreparedness to the forthcoming requirements to integrate. Social safety became a main concern in most urban communities. In the process, a subtle sense of uneasiness was already obscuring the everyday scenes. It was at the same time that Anwar found himself in Wau again seeking to establish a personal life, hoping that it would not be prejudiced by what was happening in the country. Against his expectations, everything he planned was greatly influenced.

Fear became an interred motivating force. From his inception in military, its influence has intrigued Anwar into an intractable desire to querying in the face of the unknown. He travelled the country delving into opposite ends of the story. Rendering years of his service in recognising the anecdotes with pragmatic interpretations and resolute impacts. His journeys within the North and the South though incited by acquitted impulses became an assenting pledge to his undertaking of the responsibility to effect change even in the face of the country's austere political severance. In spite knowing that these instinctive impulses were drawing him into a greater course, he believed the risk for him was worthwhile. His journey had already enticed him to the acquaintance that not probing the course would be the greatest fear of all.

Even with that clumsy beginning, he had believed that the fear of not trying would be the greatest cowardly act of a man. The men in his society are continually motivated for adventures, one after the other until one lands on the ultimate win by which one becomes recognised. Everyone has something they are known for. The ones who are not known are those who didn't make any adventure of risk-taking, for even failure in something is nerve-reckoning.

Taking action for his personal life, Anwar found that the only way was to pressure Sarah into convincing that she was better off with him in the North. Unknowingly to him, Sarah was actively planning to relocate to the newly established capital Juba.

Not knowing what the next move could be, he went to Maher in his textile shop. That part of the market has always been active with villagers arriving to get themselves new materials. The site was exuberating as every time he visited: women from different ethnicities with identical elements of prettifications beads and bright colours. He was reminded of Sarah, that girl with the looks of a villager and an intellectual mind; a sophisticated combination in a woman, he presumed. He sat watching the scuffle of buying and selling in the market until it was almost sundown. He returned home and decided he should visit Sarah, again not knowing how to get to Sarah, walking the perched space between the town and Sarah's neighbourhood. He, however, walked and reached her door in no time.

Feeling a bit hesitant after arriving, he held his hand up to knock, then put it down, turning away only to face Sarah, carrying a container full of water, returning home.

'Sarah'. He was frightened from his overthinking and her sudden appearance. He was in a state complete defeat and withdrawal from his call and aspirations. He was eager to express his desires to win her back knowing how much the renaissance of what he aspired vested on them being together.

She on the other hand was, anguished, and frightened by the devastating experiences of war and dispersal. 'Anwar?' she called.

'I hope it is not a bad time', he said.

'You tell me, is it a good time or not?' she responded with her usual protective tone. She had grown more distant and was not enthralled by many emotions anymore. Life demanded that she becomes tough. In the prime of her adult age, finding herself with her kids and having to be the breadwinner made of her an uncompromising individual.

'Am I welcome in the house, or should I just dangle around like the other time?' he said.

She placed her water flask down from her head and opened the door.

'Welcome', she said.

He helped carrying the flask into the house. That was an ice-breaking gesture. She placed a seat beside a leather-woven bed and a small coffee table. She brought a tea made with flavours of fine combinations of spices. In the savour of the time, he decided to open his heart.

'Sarah, I want to marry you and take you to the North', he said. She was quiet since she knew that Anwar talked frankly and even thoughtlessly at times. Though allured by his unremorseful and impulsive feelings, Sarah had already made her mind to move to the new capital and find a new life for herself.

'Sarah', he called her.

'Anwar, I am not the same person you met years ago. It is not okay to let you into my house this way. You are a Northerner, and I am a Southerner, and our country has divided. We are better off inside the house than at the gate. Yet that doesn't mean I have made any decision to travel with you'.

'That is why I need you in my life. I have met many people'. He became quiet, knowing this will spoil things.

'Have you met many people?' she asked as her feelings for him started to ascend.

'It's not like what you are thinking. With you, I am myself', he said, reaching for her hands and holding them tightly.

'I am not that schoolgirl anymore', she continued. 'I have my responsibilities, and I need to be up to the level of making sound decisions. I am going to Juba to search for a good-paying work'. He was quietly angered by her decision of being on a contradictory path from what he was planning. He was certain he would catch her by feelings. She had grown out of that or, rather, had perceived what was demanded of a man to earn her submission.

'Who am I to you, Sarah?' he asked with every effort to hide his shaky voice.

She was silent. Her situation demanded too much of expressions when she was already exhausted from living amidst unyielding hardships. No conversation was persuasive enough to address the reprehensions of war. His cherished recollections were crushed by the realities contradicting everything that he had hoped for. They were both in a state of vague expectations of picking the fragments of what they passionately shared from the precipice of disintegration. He was moved by seeing her plight and identifying on a reciprocal level. She stood watching as he walked away. He walked to the gate, and out he left to another day of tumbling ventures.

He arrived at the house close to midnight. He had crossed an entire woodland that he never thought imaginable even in daylight. He took a handcrafted wood chair, put it in the middle of the patio, sat on it leaning backwards with his legs spread forward and head facing the sky, gazing at the limitless stars concealing the space with shiny twinkles of illuminations that travelled beyond their time. For a while, he was drawn into contemplating what lies beyond the ordeal of time. What was divine in a journey that demanded he acted beyond his human capacity? What should he do? He has no more words to articulate his weary soul. He slumbered off on the chair until it was dawn and the *muazzin* was calling for prayer time. Maher woke for his prayers in the shed then got to the patio, only to find his poor old friend snoozing on a chair.

'Anwar', Maher called out and got to where he was and shook his shoulder to wake him. 'Where have you been?' He was quiet. 'Sarah? Do you know she is going to Juba?' Maher asked.

'What?' Anwar got off the chair. 'How did you know?' he asked, looking at Maher.

'One of my friends, a businessman, has a car that brings goods from Equatoria once in a while. He is travelling this morning'.

'What?' he yelled at him. 'Why didn't you tell me this?'

'You have not been in the house the whole day. I only learned about that yesterday evening', Maher responded.

'Can you call him to not take Sarah?' Anwar asked.

'This is out of order, Anwar. Why should I tell him that? Did you marry her?' he asked.

'There is no time for such questions. Lend me your car', Anwar said angrily.

'It has brake default. We can't drive it', Maher said. He guessed it's better to call to calm the situation. He took his phone and called. There was no response. Anwar took his phone and called Ayom. For once, he wanted the word comrade to mean trustworthy.

'Hello', Ayom responded.

'Hello. I need your car right now. There is an urgent situation', he said.

'Okay', Ayom responded without any more questioning.

Ayom tried his best to arrive as soon as possible. When he got to the house, however, it was already 6:00 a.m. Maher, on the other hand, didn't get any response from his calls.

They figured the car might have left town; all they can do was follow them on Busseri Road. The three men got on to Ayom's fine drive and took off on the red road of Busseri. Whilst the sun was rising in the auspicious of a better future, many plights have risen in people's life. There must be more to this peacetime. In few minutes, they exited the town and arrived at his previous military residence at Busseri. They had to pause there for permit. They found Kosho by the checkpoint.

'Anwar, what are you doing here?' he asked astonishingly.

'You didn't give him his woman. That's why he didn't leave', Ayom said.

'Huh, I haven't met her in a while', Kosho said.

'Do you know Sarah, Kosho?' Anwar asked.

'She is my cousin sister', Kosho responded.

'How come you never told me you knew her?' Anwar asked angrily.

'You never told me what you have with her. As her brother, I cannot comment on assumption', Kosho said.

'Now let's solve the problem', Ayom tried to fix the situation. 'She is leaving to Juba this morning'.

'Some cars just left, and I haven't seen her. Do you know which car she is taking?'

'A small passenger's car'.

'Okay, no small car has passed yet. I have been inspecting all through the dawn', he responded.

'Now, you, the two *jalaba*, stay out of sight. You don't have any authority to inspect any passing cars', Ayom said.

They entered a closed thatched shed to wait. In the extensive wait to finding Sarah in any of the passing vehicles, their discourse contemplated how their expectations have been devastated from the start of the journey into secession. Morning passed; no traces of Sarah. They asked Anwar whether to return. Anwar wanted the confirmation of a friend in deed. As they were already a couple of miles from Beringi, he asked them, 'Can we reach Beringi?'

'Let's go'. Ayom was well acquainted with such stories and was ready to go all the way.

'I am coming with you, comrades, lest you steal my sister', Kosho said, climbing on the car.

They got onto the fine drive with the radio tuned to a broadcasting on the dawn of separation. It was an era of many disjunctions. People have even separated from their individual purposes and drank to misapprehension and a sense of loss in the presence of a hard-earned subjugation of social injustice. Their search for Sarah brought them together and prompted another reality of what may come after that time.

They arrived Beringi at midday. As he expected, his good old friend Adam was there by his shop. He was surprised seeing Anwar returning at such a time. The last time he saw him was when he was deployed to Bo. 'Hej, Anwar, don tell me you voted for separation', he said.

'I was not even permitted to register, as if one vote would make a difference', Anwar responded.

'What are you doing here then?' he asked.

'Anwar is on a mission, finding his missing bride', Kosho said, walking to Adam. 'She should be taking the Awadalla's car'.

'Awadalla's car left last night', Adam said.

'What?' Anwar asked.

'There were only men in the car', Adam continued.

'Do you know the Awadallas? They have a business in town', Maher said.

'I know them very well. I get goods from them. When they got off the car, no women were on board', Adam responded.

'Are you sure?' Kosho asked.

'What? Who was on duty last night?' Adam asked. 'See, Southerners, this is what separation is bringing, so much confusion. How are you going to regulate the situation in the country? Soon you all will be accused of belonging to the *jalaba*s and be removed from your posts. Imagine what is going to happen afterwards?' he said to Kosho. Knowing the South over the years of his merchandising, Adam was too critical of the government. Nonetheless, he and many of his like felt secluded as marginalised Sudanese when the South was leaving alone.

Knowing this fact too, Kosho said, 'Don't get too much into these arguments, just watch and see what will come with time'.

'Separation is decided already, all what we have to do is drink the unpleasant cup until we could make something better', Ayom said.

'What do you think of what is happening in Juba?' Kosho asked Ayom.

'In Juba, you, me, and the *jalaba* are all one team. That's why I am saying let's just go with the current. When they begin dancing on the TV, let's just follow the move. When their moves get boring, that's when we can venture a new rhythm'.

'You are enjoying the privileges from now though', Adam said. Though a simple shop owner, Adam was a zealous, sharp thinker and totally opinionative. Many parts of the country that have been in the movement against the marginalisation have felt that they were left out at the end. They were prompted to begin forming their movements, yet which war ends all wars?

The comrades got back on board Ayom's car and started driving on the road at sunset to Wau town.

'We have to meet officially from now on, Anwar', Kosho said as he bid farewell to his friends at Busseri.

The road entering Wau was busier than ever. The drive, though, was a quiet one. The sunset painted golden grins beyond the town's symmetrical buildings.

'Now, Anwar, where to from here, Khartoum Road?' Ayom asked jokingly.

They returned to Wau. Anwar was a little composed to allow divine antecedence the rule in the course of coming events. They arrived at Maher's place and dined after a day of an unpredicted sought. The men advised Anwar to take more time and figure out what could be the next move. Against their advice, he took off at night, crossed the burren suspense, and arrived at his lover's place. He finds that Sarah has not left the town.

'I thought you left', he said when the gate was opened.

'They did not come to pick me', she said. 'Or maybe they learnt of your coming over here."

'Are you blaming me that you failed to escape this time?' he said, standing by the gate. 'Think about what I told you, I am waiting for your answer'.

'Should you come in?' Sarah asked.

'No, I am a stranger until you answer me', he said.

She was quiet again. He kissed her forehead and left. She surrendered her relegation by the abstracted turmoils of the war. She had lost members of her family and had been feeling the painful remorse of justice unattained to their cases. That day it dawned on her that her vote in the referendum was to say she had endured. For her to be attracted to a Northerner with that scale was unimaginable in her story. In her sight, he became bigger than her highest expectations and truer than the greatest of her dreams. In all inadequacy to a perfect union, their love was utopian. At the time when their country was being pulled apart, she was heartened to a deeper pursuit. Her heart began to beat in his rhythm—Anwar.

Anwar walked back, navigating the daring suspense again to get to Maher's house. The wind was extravagant with earthy smells of the creek, shrubs, and grasses. It was gentle on his face and frigid on his sweating body. The semi-wild terrain was resounding the animated subterrain tumults in the silence of the night. He crossed the precinct unapologetically.

Arriving home at almost midnight again, he found his friend Maher snoring on a chair in the place that he was sitting the other night. Dumbfounded, he pulled another chair and sat beside him, hoping that Maher's wife is not leaving town. Maher sensed his presence and walked from his sleep.

'Are you okay, Maher?' he asked.

'I should be the one asking you, where have you been?' Maher responded.

'So your family are at home?' he asked.

'Yeah, they are sleeping. My concern is you now. What should I do with you? You know what, I will set you up with one of the villagers spending the day in the veranda of my textile shop', Maher responded.

'No, I have Sarah', Anwar replied.

'She wants to go to Juba. Plus, she already looks like the villagers. So that would be a fine replacement', Maher said.

'This is not a joke', Anwar responded.

'You really love this woman, my friend', Maher said.

'You set me up with her', Anwar responded.

'What do we do now?' Maher asked.

'I have proposed', Anwar responded.

Maher was stunned by the unfolding of a love he pathetically watched fight the odds of time. He felt very significant in the process.

Who would tell that first week of Anwar's arrival to town had set the grounds for the entire course of his life? Having set his heart on Sarah, all that Maher can do was to stand by his poor friend. After all, where will they get from here? Though he chose not to ponder, he was willing to support his friend.

'Tell me what to do', he said.

Anwar nodded in fine delight. He has many to count on. He had crossed the suspense of love with triumph. Now what next?

JOURNEY TO THE BEGINNING

The North and South in Sudan have brought about one of Africa's utmost stories of social intermingling in the shattering pulls of political and economic disintegration. As a military who had set out to voice the weights of a military reign on political discords, and consequently get deployed to the Southern divisions, Anwar had watched the process of the referendum with great concern. At the time the results were announced, there was an obvious anticipated shock to both edges of the story. It became a manifested reality that up until that point, the success of the repercussion of self-determination was proportional to a more intensified process of significant reconstructions, more specifically on the social fabrics. All around the emerging state, were high hopes that in a sudden confusion, everything would be done. By whom was a daring subject to articulate. Any call for an otherwise status to self-determination was unuttered of was untimely.

Encumbered by these plights as the days were dwindling to the actual secession day, Anwar decided to have a visit downtown to be apprised of what was going around.

From the gate of the house, he could hear the propelling mill sounds drifting the busy lanes of Jaw Market. Gleaming rays stretched from the exposed merchandised utensils contoured beside the main market alleyway. He was prompted to walk into the dazzling space just in case the sight would shatter his perpetual apprehension. He walked past a busy grain shop then a series of grocery stores, then passed another main passage lined with butcheries.

He kept walking steadily out of the market, and none had stopped him for tea. Or maybe he just didn't hear anyone calling him. He walked into another road that was leading to the other side of the town. He noticed how unlike the streets of Khartoum where cars, taxis, and buses drove through out the time; in Wau, the streets were occupied only with very familiar vehicles and cargo chariots. He walked the street passing the enormous compound of the Catholic missionisers. Being in the town for many years, he couldn't help but notice how the church's presence was remarkable to the recurring advancements in the town's social structure and consistency.

He arrived at Wau Market to see Amu Mahdi. A word to describe the market was congested. Amu Mahdi was so engrossed in a newspaper he was holding, masking his sight from his surroundings. Anwar just sat on a chair quietly without intruding his meditative study. Right after his arrival, a military land rover stopped by. That was when Amu Mahdi removed the paper he was reading from his face. 'Anwar, did you arrive in that car?' he asked.

'No, I don't even own any car', he responded, picking one of the newspapers to read, to find out what was in it.

Opening the car door and getting out, marching to their direction was *liwa* Abdel Azeem, the former military commander. They watched in bewilderment, waiting to hear what brought him to them and what he was going to say. He kept marching heavily towards them.

'Salam aliekum', he began, greeting those sitting under the shed.

'Comrade', Amu Mahdi started. They have been strong associates in the town for many years. Seeing the *liwa* humbly coming to his shop at such a time was a shift of history. 'Are you looking for me?' Amu Mahdi asked jokingly and got from his chair to greet him with a hug.

'No, no, you are secure here. See how things turned around? The merchants used to seek our protection. Now we need theirs', he said laughing, greeting his good old friend with a warm embrace.

'At least you get to our level and drink tea with no orders and restrictions', Amu Mahdi responded. He had been head-to-head with the chief commander. Amu Mahdi was a very hardworking, rich, popular, and a Northerner himself. He often gets tense with *liwa*

Abdael Azeem when the military attempts to dictate his enterprises. They would meet at the main mosque week after week, whilst each one identifies and maintains their grounds. Also, as good old friends in tides of the country's surging political discords, they would resume connections time and again.

'Comrade Anwar', Abdel Azeem called Anwar's name out loudly. 'I think I should keep up with the new tone and call you comrade since you, indeed, were a comrade', he said, looking at Anwar.

Anwar had never thought that a time would approach where he would be that valuable to those he had regarded as autocrats of decision-makings in the country. At least he had a personal experience of being constricted and sent to Wau. It was time to express his feelings against how he had been dealt with by his commanders. 'Nobody heard us from the beginning'. He started talking, picking his cup of tea. 'I mean, hearing what we had to say with genuine intention of employing them when effecting orders', Anwar said.

'This has not been an empty ground, and we just arrived to establish our presence. It is part of a region shaped by historical faults and resentments. Those of you with idealistic dispositions need to understand that', *liwa* Abdel Azeem responded, looking at Anwar. 'How did you go with the commanders in the North?' he asked.

'If it was good there, I would not have resigned from military service', Anwar responded.

'You see, even there, military is military', *liwa* Abdel Azeem continued with his usual assertive tone.

'Here, you also have authority and significant influence', Anwar responded. Though knowing things were different at that point, he was too reserved for *liwa* Abdel Azeem's temperament. The least they wanted to happen was Northerners arguing over the South when it was defecting in daylight. That was what happened. Abdel Azeem was used to being in control; regardless, he didn't accept defeat. At least that had been his subconscious ventures all the past years.

'Now tell me, what happened with your story with the girl? You think they are going to allow you to take her? You are still an outsider to them after all'.

'Don't bring this story this way. She loves me, and her family have welcomed me many times in their home', Anwar objected at the mention of his personal life.

'Listen here', he started to raise his tone. 'I could have married a Southerner myself. I have all the status to make for strong proposal. The only one thing that I cannot defeat was being a Northerner', *liwa* Abdel Azeem responded.

'Any community that had experience what the Northern governments have done through the years can have a reason for justified fear considering that even when moving to the North, they weren't treated any better'. They were all quite at Anwar's defence of the people he had profoundly identified with so much that whatever he said became indisputable.

For Anwar, altruism became imperative to his ideal highest demeanour as he became one of the people sensibly guarding the decisions for secession opted by the majority of Southerners. He found that he had been consumed in the greater delineation of the wholistic narratives whilst finding himself fighting for inner contentment at the time of public amity. He was convinced that with Sarah back in his life, he could enthuse a journey to a new beginning. What was morally bestowed on him would have a devoted compatriot in a journey solely defined by sheer sacrifices. He became motivated by the need to encourage civil lobbying for the magnifying of all stories and better opportunities for all. He was convinced that amongst all his faithful fellows, Sarah was a comrade.

Amu Mahdi and Liwa Abdel Azeem have been critically entwined to pursue their individual presence in the South. From ancient times, the merchants had bonded the presence of Arabs in the region to the point that their familiarity with the South had become intrinsic. The military presence, however, is linked to domination, war, and dispersal. When governance came in place in the recent history, and the military forcefully took power, they inverted the story and projected a harsh history.

As for *liwa* Abdel Azeem, military life had modelled the entire course of his engagements. Since they must depart the town after the arrangements set in place by the peace accord, that peace time to him had snatched a whole segment of risks taken, sacrifices made, and services placed with utter precision in the name of military duty. Now he had to listen to Anwar's point of view with solemn reflection. That interval in history, empathy had the authority. Unfortunately, though it was eminently pragmatic, its application was dictated by the attitudes of wartime. That had influenced the outcome of one of the most defining events in the history of social struggles in the country and, indeed, the entire course of a nation.

Khamis returned to Wau from Juba at that time of the confusion, of finding a constructive spur to the peace process. He had to get to town for another important reason: Sarah's wedding to Anwar. It was a simple traditional banquet to honour their beautiful union. Though actively involved in nation-building process of the new state, Khamis was their strongest supporter. He had been a man in sought of human dignity. He believed that at some point, a mutual discourse would command a new pattern in the story of struggle in the country.

'Be good to each other, the North is never far from the South', he advised them. Being 'never far' was a characteristic depiction of family relations, indicating that conventional social ties are not part of the separation.

On the day of secession, Anwar and Sarah watched with sheer anticipation the birth of a new nation, a nation they belonged to indistinctively. Anwar had a distinctive realization of how resilience and the consistent recounting of a just cause would eventually pay off at some point. Like a love story, the lover would ultimately submit, and love would overcome.

So much had been morally bestowed on Anwar and Sarah in their individual journeys. The traces of their actions on the opposing ends of the story had combined in a tender banner that would eventually inspire an entire generation to imagine a time beyond war. They became charged with a deeper responsibility to seek the attainment of individual peace across their associations. Their profound revelation was that what connects humanity is beyond wars or socio-political definitions.

'Why can't we remain in the South?' Sarah asked.

Anwar looked at her, caressed her face without hesitation, and said, 'Every fraction to us is homeland'.

Lightning Source UK Ltd.
Milton Keynes UK
UKHW040733061022
409941UK00017B/140/J